THE MESSENGER

(MORTAL BELOVED, BOOK ONE)

PAMELA DUMOND

PAMELA DUMOND MEDIA

Dedication

Melissa Black Ford

True friends from High School to Old School.

Thank you and love you, forever.

ABOUT THE MESSENGER

PRAISE for THE MESSENGER

"**gritty and gorgeous**" A. Reviewer

"All the excitement of **OUTLANDER** if it was a YA series!" A. Reviewer

"... by the end, I was getting **a bicep workout from all the fistpumps...** I'm dying to hear the rest of the story it started telling me right at the end of the night." ForeverYoungAdult Review

"**This book held me captive** because not only did it have time traveling in it but it had Native American history... a magical story with lots of twists and turns... " A Diary of a Book Addict Blog

"For those who like **The Immortals series by Alyson Noel**, Timeless by Alexandra Monir, or The Eternal Ones by

Kirsten Miller – The Messenger is a must read." Breathe in
Books Blogspot

"DuMond is a superlative writer who sets the stage for an
historical romantic adventure, and then fiendishly leaves
the reader hanging at the end. " Midwest Book Review,
Shelley Glodowski

DESCRIPTION

A boy from the past. A girl from the future. Their love could be
forever, but their time is running out...

Madeline falls in love with Samuel when she accidentally
time travels hundreds of years into the past. Their relationship is forbidden. Samuel's half Native and Madeline's white.
Every rendezvous they share must be secret. If discovered
they could be brutally punished.

But Madeline's traveled to the past not only to fall in love,
but also to claim her birth right as a Messenger, a soul who
can slip through time's fabric, delivering messages that
change one life, or save many. Deadly Hunters, dark-souled
time travelers, crave her powers and seek to seduce or
kill her.

Can Madeline find her way back to the future in time to save
herself and Samuel?

Continue reading Madeline and Samuel's saga in...

THE ASSASSIN (#2) and THE SEEKER (#3) and THE
BELIEVER (#4) : *Jack & Clara*

WATCH

The Messenger Mortal Beloved Book Trailers!

Mortal Beloved Messenger Sizzle Reel

The Messenger Book Trailer

PROLOGUE

 low-pitched droning penetrated my ears and rattled my bones. Being a city girl, I usually didn't care about a little noise. Could be an L train whistling nearby outside my bedroom window, a bus chugging down the street, or a garbage truck picking up trash on any normal day. But it wasn't any of those, 'cause this day definitely wasn't normal.

I tore through a thick wood, my breath ragged, as skinny tree branches whipped across my face and body. One slapped my forehead and something warm trickled into my eye. I wiped it away and saw that my hand was bloody. I should be used to that by now.

But I flinched and tried not to cry out in pain because *he* was hunting me. If he heard me, he could calculate how far away I was, and then he would be able to easily catch me. If he caught me, he would kill me.

But I didn't want to die, yet. Not here, not now. I had to find a way to be with my Samuel.

I started running again, but this time shielded my face

PAMELA DUMOND

with my arms. My feet kicked up some dirt as well as a few yellow and orange leaves blanketing the ground.

I fled past ancient pine trees with thick, round trunks and branches covered with needles that towered over me like a canopy, when I tripped on the hem of my skirt. I heard a loud rip as I fell toward the forest floor. My arms pin wheeled and momentum—possibly the only thing on my side right now—jerked me upright.

I stopped for a few seconds to catch my breath. The droning had grown louder. Good. I was closer to that place where desire, action, a little bit of luck, and magic would join forces. I'd find that moment to slip through time's fabric, travel hundreds of years back to present day and warn or even save people—especially my Samuel.

Then I heard *his* muffled voice close by and his words chilled my soul. "Stop running, Messenger," he said. "You cannot save him or yourself. You cannot save anybody."

I'm sixteen-years-old and cop to the fact that in terms of life wisdom, people thought teenagers had been through next to nothing. But I've recently learned the hard way that I wasn't your average teenager and wisdom cannot be measured in birthdays.

CHAPTER 1

$\mathcal{I}$ stood close to the front of the #4 Chicago bus and clutched one of the thin metal poles with both of my hands. It was an early morning, standing-room-only commute, packed primarily with people on their way to work. Five days out of every school week, this was my ride to high school. I had the route memorized, so I knew when to squeeze my eyes shut, count to thirty in my head, and remind myself to breathe through my fear.

Once in a while I'd open my eyes too early and we'd still be on the overpass that towered so high above the roads below it, that a simple fender bender could be deadly. It was ten years ago today that Mama and I were in a car accident, and I still had a fear of heights.

This time my fear wasn't simply Anxiety-related. A recent study confirmed that more than two thousand Illinois bridges and overpasses were "structurally deteriorated," severely cracked, and could crumble at any time—and this fifty-year-old overpass was one of them.

We made it to the other side and the driver maneuvered the bus into its stop on the corner. There was a 'Whoosh' when he pushed the button that opened the doors. I let everybody who was in a hurry push past me and exit first. I didn't want to bump anyone, or get tripped myself. My phone buzzed. I pulled it out of my purse and saw another text from Brett, my kind-of-boyfriend.

"Need to talk."

His texts were making me nervous. We hadn't seen each other a lot over the summer. Brett went to Future Leaders of America in Washington, D.C., where he hung out at Congressional hearings, partied with lobbyists, and interned with a Chicago congressman.

I worked three part-time jobs: read books to my ancient neighbor, walked her surly mop of a dog, and changed litter boxes at a local animal rescue. But now it was fall, we were both juniors at Preston Academy, and hopefully our relationship was back on track.

I crossed the wide, yellowing lawn that made its way from the sidewalk to a large, solid, brick building. The late September wind kicked up. Colored leaves swept off the trees and hurtled through the air around the four story, one hundred plus year old structure that had been a printing warehouse south of Chicago's downtown, but now housed my high school.

A tall, chunky, weathered limestone marker embedded in the ground in front read: "Preston Academy. Founded in 1896. Transforming Today's Youth into Tomorrow's Leaders."

I joined a loud, chatty crowd of about three hundred teens of multiple nationalities and skin colors descended on our school's enormous, ancient, pitch-black, wooden front doors.

"Yo, Madeline," a guy called. "Wait up!"

I spotted Aaron: cute, sixteen, and metro, hustling through the crowds toward me. He wore an "Autumn in

Connecticut" ensemble I'd seen recently in the front window of Banana Republic's flagship store on Michigan Avenue.

He wrapped his arm around mine. Cozy. "What's with the extra beauty exertion, blondie?" he asked.

"Brett texted me. Said we needed to talk."

Aaron made a face. "Could you pick someone a little more vanilla to be semi-dating?"

"Brett's cute and fun and… well you're looking a little prepped out yourself, dude," I said. "You're practically Ivy-League bound."

Aaron smiled. "More like an actor wannabe guide on top of an 'Explore Chicago!' Tour Bus." He pointed West. "And that, my friend is where Mrs. O'Leary's cow kicked over the bucket which started the great Chicago Fire. Maybe the Bears could recruit that cow for their offensive line." He laughed, which normally would have made me laugh, too.

Today I barely cracked a smile. "Since when have you liked football?"

"Hot men grappling each other in the name of sport," he said. "What's there not to like?"

"Why are you always so chilled, Aaron? How do you do it?"

"Years of practice. People have been making fun of me since I was a kid. I combat the energy suckers with humor."

We walked through the front doors of our school and entered an enormous limestone-floored foyer with a ridiculously tall ceiling. There were skylights made of stained glass mosaics depicting historical events and persons like Joan of Arc. Other mosaics featured lesser-known people—like Zenobia of Syria, a female warrior who defeated legions of Roman soldiers.

The foyer's walls were lined floor-to-ceiling with pale rose and terra cotta shaded bricks dated and autographed by every person who graduated Preston Academy. A sleek, tall, library-style ladder rested in the corner of the room should someone want to push it around the foyer's walls and climb it to see one of the grad's signatures, up close and personal.

There was also a stack of small, expensive, hand-woven rugs donated by a well-known local artist, (another Preston alum) for people whose relatives had bricks located toward the bottom of the walls. They could sit or kneel on a rug and cushion their body parts while they examined their loved one's signature.

I stared up at one brick close to the ceiling. There was no way I'd ever climb that ladder or touch that brick—especially not today.

I walked toward a doorway that siphoned off the massive foyer into what looked like an average, high school hallway lined with lockers, chatty students, and classroom doors.

———

My history class was packed with twenty-eight people. Our desks were old, small, and scribbled on. The room smelled musty, probably from the molding maps, ancient newspaper and magazine articles covering the walls from floor to ceiling detailing different times and places. Or maybe 'cause the gym's locker room was just down the hall.

"Who penned the famous phrase, "Those who don't know history are doomed to repeat it'?" Mr. Stanley Preston, my teacher, asked from the front of the room. He was forty-something with dyed auburn hair and leaned against a wide blackboard while he munched on a gooey Danish with a napkin underneath.

Taylor Smythe—smart, pretty, and the recent recipient of a perfect nose job by the third best plastic surgeon in Chicago—touched her nose and raised her hand.

Mr. Preston nodded at her. "Ms. Smythe?"

"The Greek warrior who conquered Troy," Taylor said. She swished her hair back and touched her nose again. Like her new nose had turned into a lucky rabbit's foot with magical powers.

Mr. Preston crumpled the napkin and tossed it toward the wastebasket next to his desk. It missed and landed on the floor. He wiped his hands and a few crumbs flew through the air. "A for effort, Ms. Smythe." He stuck his chin out and rubbed it with one hand.

He probably saw someone do that in a movie and thought it made him look smart.

I thought it made him look like a chin molester.

"Actually, those words were written by famous philosopher, George Santayana, published in the year 1905 in a book called, *The Flux and Constancy in Human Nature.*"

Taylor waved her hand in the air in front of him like she was the princess on a homecoming float. Mr. Preston nodded at her. "That was my second guess, Mr. Preston," she said and batted her eyes.

He smiled and sauntered down one of the classroom's aisles. Thankfully, not mine. "I wish more of your fellow classmates shared your high regard for history, Ms. Smythe, as well as your willingness to participate in class."

Twenty of my fellow prisoners—I mean classmates— fidgeted and stared down at their desks, the ceiling, or each other while they doodled on their binders. Five students were actually into history and either tolerated or brown-nosed our teacher, a direct descendent of our school's founder.

One student—me—was completely distracted because I hadn't talked to Brett and something didn't feel right. I bit my nails.

Mr. Preston slammed his small, puffy hand onto my desk

and leaned his sweaty face into mine. "Not a pretty habit, Ms. Blackford. I have a question for you."

I felt my ears turn red. "Yes, Mr. Preston?" The entire class perked up and eyeballed me. Apparently, current drama was more interesting than historical.

"It's simple. I want you to answer my *last question*." He smiled at me, his small mouth jammed with tiny, pointed teeth.

My best friend Chaka Silverman, a gorgeous, mocha teen with heaps of multi-colored braids, gestured to me behind Preston's back. She pointed to the blackboard.

I squinted at it. Thanks for the tip, Chaka, but I still didn't know the answer.

"Name and describe one of the biggest land grabs in the history of the North American continent."

So I guessed. "When President Bush's people stole the presidency from Mr. Gore in the 2004 elections? Does the voter conspiracy in Florida that year count as a land grab?" I asked, and heard half the students groan. Preston Academy wasn't just a school for liberals' kids.

"Technically, no." Mr. Preston frowned. "Might I add, many people do not believe for a second that President Bush's people stole that election. Besides, that subject is covered in your American Government class." He held his fingers up in the air in mock horror. "Thank God, as I hate touching on subjects that are recent, scandalous, or fiercely debated."

He glanced around the room. Stood taller, puffed out his chest, and ambled past students' desks. His energy emanated from my desk into my body and I felt slimed.

"I was a *student* at Preston Academy before I became a *teacher* here," he said. "I guarantee that you will get nowhere in life unless you learn history's lessons, and what they offer you." He turned toward me like a hungry coyote eyeing a tiny dog mistakenly left outside after dusk. "We are still anxiously awaiting your real answer."

I felt my face flush. "Um… I don't know. Yet. I'll do the homework and find out."

"But that *was* the homework. Which you seemed to forget."

Taylor laughed along with a couple of her minion friends.

Chaka stuck her bejeweled arm up in the air and waved it around, her bangles jangling. "Mr. Preston?"

"Yes, Ms. Silverman?"

"This semester's only been happening for three weeks. So my very smart girl here," Chaka pointed at me, "really isn't all that behind. We haven't even had a test or a major paper due yet. You, Mr. Preston, are a descendent of Emily Preston. She was a pioneer in education as well as a role model for all of us, which makes me think that you're a reasonable man. I know that you'll give all of us juniors a fair chance to fail or succeed based on our merits and not judge us on one, bad day."

Stanley Preston's eyes narrowed. "Noted, Ms. Silverman."

The bell rang.

"Class dismissed," he said.

Phew. Good job, Chaka. The entire class pushed back our chairs and scrambled to leave.

"A twenty-page term paper is due next week on Friday." He smacked his lips. "Subject: Major land grabs in America's history."

The students groaned.

Mr. Preston gestured innocently. "Thank Ms. Silverman. It was her idea."

Chaka shot him her You-Will-Die-Fool look, which she reserved for major losers on special occasions.

I was almost out the door and headed toward tracking down Brett.

"Ms. Blackford, stay behind for a moment. We need a word," he said.

No, we didn't. Not today. Not now. My fellow students pushed past me out the door.

Chaka lingered. "I'll wait for you," she mouthed as she eased out the door.

CHAPTER 2

*M*r. Preston closed the door between our classroom, the hallway, and probably my sanity. I stood next to his desk filled with comic books, real books, and magazines. A grayish rock veined with white-quartz crystal that was bigger than my fist rested on a bunch of papers, and functioned as a paperweight.

"Madeline." He ambled to his desk. "Just because your family has influential friends and you retain a partial scholarship here, does not mean you can afford to slack off or slide. At any moment you can be dismissed from Preston Academy for bad grades and/or attitude issues." He picked up a stack of magazines and tapped them on his desk to align them.

A weathered copy of *Maxim* poked out from the stack. Ew.

"Frankly, I believe you are pushing the boundaries with both of these concerns." He pushed that magazine back into the paper pile.

"You wanted to know if we had any ideas or thoughts

about land grabs. Right now, I don't have a great answer. But, Mr. Preston, I will research and report back."

His smile turned to a frown. "Do that by this Monday, please."

Great. There went my weekend. When my cell phone vibrated, I glanced and jumped when I saw Brett's number. My heart pounded and my foot tapped on the floor almost all on its own. "Mr. Preston, can I answer this? It's important."

"Preston Academy has a strict policy that all phones are turned off during class," he said. "Surely, you know that."

My phone hummed—Brett was on the line; my love life was on the line—but not for much longer. "Technically we're between classes," I pleaded.

"May I?" He smiled and held out his hand toward my phone.

I handed it to him and he examined it. "Oh, dear. Your phone seems to be an older model." He frowned. "One that loses signals easily." He pushed a button and Brett's call disappeared.

I closed my eyes and bit my lip, trying to hold my temper.

"Lip biting, like nail chewing, is another unattractive habit." He leaned closer to me.

The smell of his cheap cologne drifted up my nose. It took everything in my being not to move away from him. Good thing I didn't eat breakfast, as that would be coming up right about now.

"Phone calls might seem important. But honestly, it's up to you," he said. "When you're in the middle of a teacher-student conference regarding your lackluster academic performance, you need to determine whether a phone call from a young man might be worth dropping a grade, detentions, or even stepping *off* the fast-track to a reputable college."

"I know that, Mr. Preston." I looked up at the large clock on the wall behind his desk. "Can we please continue this later, sir?" I spotted Chaka pointing at her watch through the small window in the classroom's door. "I've got about five minutes to get to gym class, change clothes, and be on time."

"Well that's a class you certainly don't want to flunk." He handed my phone back to me.

I bolted out the door into the hallway.

"Why is Piranha Preston so pissed at you?" Chaka asked, her signature bangles jangling as we raced down the hall.

"I don't have a flippin' clue. I just want to get in the water and swim," I said. "I love the water. It clears my head."

"I hate swimming," Chaka said. "Unless it's on Dad's island in the Caribbean; the water's crystal clear and bathwater warm. Not to mention the pool boys fight over who's going to teach me how to snorkel."

"You have your diving certificate, Chaka." I slammed open the door to the girls' locker room.

She giggled. "Who cares? They're really hot, and don't know that."

After gym class Chaka had a date with study hall, and I had to find Brett. I returned to the foyer with Aaron at my side. If Brett was actually in Preston Academy today, this was probably the best place to find him.

People from all over the world traveled to see and experience Preston Academy's famous foyer. They came to make etchings from the signatures of their loved ones, or the grads that became celebrities. Recently, a young, über successful, popstar received permission to film parts of her music video for her newest platinum hit in the famous foyer—following a hefty donation to our school's scholarship fund, of course—and spotlighted her mom's autographed brick. A couple of Preston students were in the video. I wasn't one of them.

I had seen these foyer walls so often that my eyes skipped over the famous people: the politicians (local and national), the actors, and the wealthy entrepreneurs. Instead, my eyes came to rest, like they did every time I walked through these doors, on one autograph.

"Rebecca Wilde" was inscribed on a brick high on the wall, well over my head and out of reach. I squinted up at her name on the wall.

"Your mother and I were in the same class," Mr. Preston said. "Rebecca was a risk-taker. Very different from you, Madeline."

I swiveled and saw him standing just a few yards behind me.

"What's his problem?" Aaron hissed.

"In fact," Mr. Preston said, "I heard Rebecca climbed rickety scaffolding on a dare to cement that brick up there, herself. She got in a bit of trouble for that, though. Someone turned her in."

"Probably him," Aaron whispered. "I'll pull the ladder over. Climb it and touch her signature."

I hesitated. Aaron walked toward that stupid ladder, kneeled next to its base and flipped down the floor locks. He leaned one shoulder against it, and wheeled it around the foyer's walls until he parked it under mama's brick. He beckoned, "Come on."

I froze, surrounded, bombarded, by teens hurrying in multiple directions. Everyone was moving except for me. It dawned on me that I was completely caught in time; *I was the girl who couldn't move.*

The top of the ladder appeared like it stretched to the sky. I hated heights, and this whole scene was too tall, too stress-inducing, too much. Which made me wonder if I had my stash of anti-anxiety pills in my purse. I usually didn't need them. But every once in a while, I'd have a full-blown panic attack, which would leave me paralyzed.

Aaron patted the ladder. "It's not that high up. If you were a rock-climber or enjoyed mountains and cliffs, this ladder would be like a stepstool. It would be nothing."

When I was twelve, my family and I celebrated my step-mom, Sophie, getting hired as a legal assistant at O'Ryan and Sons. We nibbled on tapas in the middle of a trendy restaurant called Barcelona, which was on the first floor, no heights involved—whatsoever. I heard the screech of tires braking, and a loud 'BANG,' from a nearby car crash. The next thing I knew, I lay on the floor in Child's Pose, my head between my knees.

I was drenched in sweat and struggled to breathe for fifteen minutes. I clasped my hands over my ears while my dad and Sophie knelt on the floor with me. They hugged me and whispered that everything would be okay; it all would be fine, really. But out of the corners of my eyes I caught the stares of pity from fellow diners, as well as the embarrassed glances from the waiters. We haven't been back to that restaurant since.

"Your mama's brick is about eighteen feet up. You can do eighteen feet." Aaron said.

Mr. Preston smiled and shook his head. "She's too busy waiting for a phone call."

Aaron glared at me and snapped his fingers.

"Fine!" I clasped my hands behind my back, stretched my shoulders wide-open, and stomped my feet on the floor, twice. I climbed a few steps up the ladder and looked down at Aaron. "You need to hold onto the bottom of this thing in case someone bumps into us."

He grabbed onto the ladder's railings and planted his feet. "I'm here. Call me Elmer. Climb."

So I did. I climbed two more steps. Five steps. About ten feet up I began to hyperventilate a little. I managed a few more rungs. About thirteen feet up I clutched my chest with one hand, and my breath turned raspy. "You're holding that ladder tight? You're not going to let it slip?" Sweat dripped off my palms as I squeezed the railings.

"We're good," Aaron encouraged.

It felt like I was climbing through mud, but I made it up three more steps. I was about fifteen feet up. If I climbed just three more feet, I could stretch my arm high over my head and touch mama's brick. I never in my wildest dreams planned on doing this, and until now, never even thought it possible.

Sudden warmth enveloped me and my skin tingled. The logical part of my brain kicked in and explained that since I was so high up, close to the foyer's ceiling, heat rises to the top. There were only floor heaters in this room, but they hadn't yet been fired up and weren't usually turned on until around Halloween.

I always thought if I ever found myself this high off the earth again, that I'd feel light-headed. But instead, I felt grounded. Didn't make any sense. I was about a yard away from touching the actual brick that mama helped create. Once I placed my hand on her signature, maybe I could feel in my own body what Rebecca felt in hers, while she was a student here. Perhaps I could feel what darkness filled her heart and made her so callous about abandoning me.

"You're doing great." Aaron's voice broke. "Don't look down. You're close, like that guy who climbed Everest or something. Or that guy who had his hand trapped... but they made a movie about him. James Franco, the actor, was totally hot and…"

Aaron was talking gibberish, and I was an idiot, so of course I looked down. I saw Brett O'Ryan, my kind-of boyfriend, walking on the foyer far below me. His arm was wrapped tight around the shoulders of a petite girl with porcelain skin and long, curly, red hair. WTH? My hands started shaking.

Aaron's eyes flitted between Brett and me. He smacked one of his palms onto his forehead and frowned. "I said don't look… Aw, Maddie. Could you take directions from anyone, just once?"

I gripped the ladder's railings 'til my fingers turned white and shook my head. "No." I glared at Brett. No need for any more texts; I'd figured out his news. "Hey, Brett!"

They looked up at me. Brett's face blanched. The girl he was with? Her perfect face was smooth, porcelain, and stone blank. Not blank, like she was dumb. Just empty, like something I couldn't quite put my finger on it. And right now, my heart was too crushed to even try to figure it out.

Brett shifted from one foot to another. He smoothed his white-blonde hair back from his forehead with his free hand. "Hey, uh, Maddie. I've been trying to get a hold of you about that, um, project." He looked down, and coughed into his free hand—the hand that wasn't wrapped around that girl's shoulder.

He peered back up at me: huddled and hanging for dear life fifteen feet up in the air, on a stupid ladder. "Can we talk later, buddy?"

"Buddy?" I asked. With the exception of Aaron and Chaka, I'd shared more secrets with Brett than anyone else. We knew each other for years. Had confided in each other for hours in his house, grungy coffee shops, in city parks, on Lake Michigan's beaches, on the dunes in Indiana as we huddled beneath some pine trees high in the hills, while the winds whipped past us creating mini-sandstorms.

We went to some Junior High dances and Preston Academy events. We also shared some kissing action. Now he was practically breathing down the neck of a girl who happened to be a dead ringer for Miss Teen Ireland, and I was "Buddy?"

"Absolutely. Later." I looked Brett in his eyes. He couldn't hold my gaze for longer than a second, and my heart sunk as I realized I was *never* in Brett's heart the way I wanted to be. And frankly—that sucked—'cause I had liked him for a very long time.

"Uh, great. Thanks," Brett said and walked away with that gorgeous girl glancing up at me while she whispered into his ear.

I felt my heart twist and sink into my stomach. I stared at the ground below me. It looked about a hundred feet down—not fifteen. The room spun. I clung to the ladder's railing, plunked my butt down onto a ladder stair, and tucked my head under my arm.

"Hold onto this thing!" Aaron said to someone, way off in a fog somewhere. "Hang on, Madeline. I'm coming to get you."

CHAPTER 3

I don't know how, exactly, but Aaron got me down off that ladder and somehow dragged me to the school cafeteria.

Chaka had rolled out her yoga mat, and I lay in Child's Pose on it for I-have-no-idea how long, before I was able to lift my head off the ground.

"Take this." Aaron shoved a tiny, white pill at me.

I swallowed it.

"Drink this." Chaka thrust a water bottle at me.

My hands shook as I struggled to unscrew the top.

Aaron grabbed the bottle, yanked the top off and handed it back. "You'll feel better in no time."

I chugged the water and dropped the bottle. "I'll feel better when I talk to my mama."

I was six-years-old and strapped into a booster seat in the back of Mama's dinged hatchback while she drove to an important appointment after my horseback-riding lesson. I didn't know what the important appointment was about—didn't care—'cause I was hanging with Mama, which was always a good thing.

We were driving in one of those tall parking garages, the kind that was round like a soup can, where the ramp spiraled up—which felt like we were going in circles. The last thing I remembered was our car accelerating like crazy, me getting dizzy and asking Mama to slow down. Then there was a loud BANG! That's it.

Now, I sat on the concrete ground on the tenth floor of the same circular, open-aired parking garage that featured moderately priced apartments above it. They were moderate, because while the building overlooked water, it wasn't a postcard view of Lake Michigan but a grimy, skinny branch of the Chicago River that trickled past in the near distance.

I leaned back against a cold, concrete, support pillar about twelve feet from the sturdy, coiled, metallic rope that connected more columns in front of me. A chilly wind sliced through my hair, and I shivered. The rope separated this solid structure from the open air surrounding it. The thickness and metal design of the rope were intended to keep vehicles from catapulting off the edges of the garage. That worked most of the time.

My butt was numb from the cold concrete, and I hoped my jeans and T-shirt didn't absorb the garage floor's oil stains, discarded cigarettes, or the spray-painted, gang graffiti tags on the pillar that I leaned against. I shivered again, and hugged myself.

I'd bolted from Preston Academy without my coat and was wearing only a paper-thin, long-sleeved T-shirt in fifty-degree weather. My cheeks were undoubtedly stained with mascara rings, and I probably looked awful. But really, who cared?

I craned my neck forward, and checked out the vacant lot

below the parking structure. It was a sad sight: a large patch of weeds littered with trash and junk that had been dumped in the river had found their home here—most likely after a storm got wild enough to toss them onto the riverbanks.

Aside from the newer makes and models of the neatly parked cars, ten years after the accident, this whole scene still looked pretty much the same. Except this time I wasn't strapped into the back seat of a car, hanging by its rear tires caught on the safety wire, ten stories off this ledge, suspended between sky and ground, life and death. And, according to the police report and descriptions from several witnesses who raced to the scene, screaming my lungs out.

I guess it's good I had no memories of the actual accident. Amnesia, post-traumatic stress, whatever—I'd blacked it all out. I woke up on a skinny mattress in a tiny, antiseptic-smelling hospital bay in the emergency room, with wires hanging off me, while Dad peered completely panic-stricken into my face.

At that point, Mama was only missing two hours. Dad probably thought she escaped the wreck, and wandered off, dazed. Too bad we'd never seen or heard from her again. Where had she gone? Why had she left?

Over the years I learned enough about our accident by overhearing what people slipped in conversations, as well as what I googled. The police investigated, but never found the car, or the driver who rammed us. They never found my mama; suspected she used the accident as a 'Get Out of Jail Free,' card. Escaped her life as a mom and wife to start some-place new.

Dad never bought that. But after she'd been gone two years, he gave into mama's family's request and had her declared dead, so she could be officially mourned. Eventually, people pretty much forgot I was that poor girl whose mom disappeared. I was able to introduce myself without getting socked with questions, or the all-too-familiar looks loaded with pity.

So, sitting here now back at the scene, I didn't know whether to feel surprised, shocked, or nothing. Between getting dumped by Brett, the possibility of losing my scholarship to Preston Academy, and having a panic attack—today was awful.

I thought that if I had the courage to return to the scene of our accident and sit for a while, perhaps even tried to meditate or pray, I would remember what happened. Then I could have less fear, and feel more peaceful—and be able to climb a stupid ladder. But the only things I felt right now were confusion, and a heavy ache in my chest.

I looked around the parking structure and noticed a bunch of gang tags painted onto the concrete, next to newer model cars. Apparently people weren't scared to park here. They'd probably never even heard of the accident that happened ten years ago, in this very spot.

What was I thinking? That she'd show up and explain why she left ten years ago? That she'd drop off a box of chocolates with an, *'I'm sorry I abandoned you,'* note? I'd been here for a couple of hours, and other than the obvious outcome—my lips were probably blue and my fingernails definitely white—I hadn't gained anything by coming back.

I rubbed my hands together, held them to my mouth and blew on them. I wondered what my life would have looked like, felt like, if Mama had never disappeared. Frankly, the only person I would have missed, would be my stepmom, Sophie.

I heard a jangle of keys and an older guy said, "Hey, kid. You look cold. Need a ride?"

I looked up at the man who belonged to the voice. He was late forties, handsome, full head of dark hair, thin, and tall. He walked up the ramp toward me wearing crisp khakis, and a fine, dark brown, weathered, leather, bomber jacket. I heard the low, throaty hum of a finely tuned car engine in the distance—probably his ride.

"No, thanks." I waved him on.

"I'd believe you except that your fingers are purple." He held out his right hand in front of me. "Look at mine. Wow. They're a normal fleshy color."

"Kudos on your great circulation," I said.

"Look. Whatever your beef is, you need to get out of the cold, call your folks, and talk it out." The guy reached in his pocket and held his cell phone out toward me.

I shook my head. "I'm fine."

"Right. If you don't want to talk to them yet, at least find someplace safe to stay tonight. I can recommend a couple of shelters."

"It's not what you think." I heard a high-pitched, grating sound, and some lame car backfired a couple of times. Busted. Dad drove his beater ride, and huffed up the garage incline toward me.

He screeched to a stop in the middle of the ramp, yanked the parking brake, flung open the driver's door and catapulted out. The keys were in the ignition, engine still running, as he raced toward me with his longish, salt and pepper hair flying all over the place.

"Daddy?"

"You stay away from her!" Dad thrust one arm out at the guy in the bomber jacket and shook his fist at him.

The guy stared at my dad like he was crazy, but took the hint. "Just trying to help." He walked back down the ramp. The smooth engine revved below us—the guy must have had a friend behind the wheel of his ride.

"We don't need help from strangers." Dad strode after the guy determined, almost manic.

"Dad, no!" I pushed myself off the ground, and ran after

23

him. "I'm fine." I grabbed his arm. His eyes met mine and they were a little crazy, reminding me of the old days after the accident. Guess I wasn't the only one having a hard time today. "This man did nothing wrong." I shook his arm.

But his eyes were dilated, and he was breathing quickly. Dad was in his crazy zone, and I had to break through to him before he did something he'd get in trouble for. I could not lose him again. "He was just trying to help," I said. Dad's nostrils flared. "Leave him alone. You cannot fight everyone." I tugged on the sleeve of his jean jacket.

He sighed and closed his eyes for a moment. When he re-opened them, he appeared sane.

"Okay," he said. "If you recall, I had a rotator cuff injury on that arm you're yanking on. I'd really appreciate it if you stopped doing that."

"Sorry." I patted his shoulder.

"Much better."

The man regarded us. "I didn't come here for a fight, sir. I spotted your daughter and, well, I have a teenager. Stuff happens. I just wanted to make sure she was okay."

"I'm sorry, man," Dad replied. "I apologize."

"No worries." The man turned and continued down the ramp.

Dad wrapped his arms around me and squeezed so hard I coughed. "You're catching a cold! You shouldn't have come here." He wiped a tear from his eye. "Darn, now I'm catching that cold."

I hugged him back. Was this the first time we really connected since Mama disappeared? Dad smoothed my hair, over and over. It felt strange coming from him. But it also felt really good. "What were you thinking?" he asked.

"I thought if I came back here, talked to Mama... Maybe I could find a way to remember?"

"You don't need to remember," he said. "I'm glad you

don't remember. I can't lose anyone else right now." He pulled off his jean jacket and handed it to me. "Put this on before you catch pneumonia."

"You will never lose me," I said. "As long as we can order Joey's Pizza Super Combo Deluxe for dinner. Extra large, so Sophie and Jane can have some."

He frowned. "Ack, Joey's! White flour carbohydrates topped with decrepit vegetables with zero nutritional value, and do you even remember what I told you about how they kill cows?" We walked the few feet to his car, and opened the passenger door. "Jane has a sleepover, and Sophie's leaving on a business trip."

"Again?" I asked.

"Yes, but we decided you're getting your big present tonight." Dad pulled his cell out of his pocket and made a call. "Pick-up. I want the insecticide pizza deluxe. Yes, I meant the super deluxe combo." He pointed to me. "Happy? Get in."

CHAPTER 4

*I*slumped in a spindly, antique, hand-carved, wooden chair in my parents' study. I managed to catch Sophie before she headed out on yet another business trip. She gave me a big hug and a smooch on my cheek. She was more affectionate toward me right now than she was toward my dad.

They were going through a rough patch, and arguing about how much time Sophie was out of town for work. Dad was a chiropractor and his business, like many small businesses, was a little slow right now. Sophie took every gig that would pay overtime.

I felt awful, completely wiped out from today's events. "I'm not hungry. Can I go? Can we do this tomorrow night?" I asked.

"You will eat some pizza, absorb whatever nutrition can be garnered from that slop, and be happy about it." Dad kneeled on the floor, his head all the way under an antique desk. "Besides, I am retrieving your present. And, it's a big one."

"I can stay ten more minutes."

"You'll stay until I hand you your present."

I gnawed on a slice of pizza, and looked around the room. It was pretty small, dusty, and from what I remembered— used to be magical. That was when it was Mama's office.

As a kid I'd sit on the floor with a puzzle or a coloring book, while she hunched over her desk, eyeglasses perched halfway down her nose squinting at her computer, shuffling through papers on her desk, and writing on them. She'd get up and draw lines in different colors on huge, white boards that leaned against the walls. Then she'd lean in, and scribble words next to the lines.

The last time I hung out in her office was when I was six. She was working away, while I sprawled on a little throw carpet on the floor, reading a new book.

Dad hollered from down the hall, "Rebecca! Need some help for a second, please?"

Mama looked up from her papers, stood up and headed toward the door. I hated for our time together to be over. "Are the lines for a new puzzle, Mama?"

"Good question." She hugged me. That felt so great I decided to ask good questions more often.

"Rebecca!" Dad yelled.

"Coming, Ray!" Mama smiled at me while I pouted. "I'm hoping all the lines I'm drawing will help me solve a very big puzzle. And soon, my gifted daughter Madeline, I will teach you what *your* piece of that puzzle is." She caressed my hair, leaned in, and kissed me on my forehead. Then she walked out of the room.

"I'm a puzzle piece, Mama?" I yelled. "For real?" But she was gone.

Ten years later, I picked on a piece of pizza in her former office. It was lined with bookshelves packed with books, papers, notebooks, boxes, and a few framed photos covered in dust. Unlike the rest of our free-for-all, aging hippie house

—the door to this room was always locked. Being invited in here meant that it was a special occasion, or a scary one. I was hoping for the former, but after today—couldn't rule out the latter.

Dad knelt on the floor next to Mama's old wooden desk that had too many drawers to count. A Joey's pizza box rested next to it on a cheap card table specially set up for this event. A greasy pizza box would not be allowed to lie on Mama's antique desk.

I heard scrapes and scratches and a few cuss words as Dad fiddled with something. "Darn! It's been so long since we last unlocked this thing. Sorry. It's just not opening," he said and jammed something that sounded metallic into the desk's underbelly.

"I think you need pizza. Sustenance." I tore off a piece from the pie, put it on a paper towel, and waved it around near the bottom of the desk.

He twisted half his body around, poked his arm out, and handed me an ancient, worn skeleton key. "Put that in the front desk drawer next to the paperclips." He took the pizza and munched. "Thanks for the dreck. I'm starving."

He pulled a Swiss Army Knife out from his rear jeans pocket, flipped open one of those weird attachments, and finagled it into the lock that lay underneath the desk.

"Hello," Dad said in a deep voice. "My name's Dr. Raymond Blackford, Chiropractor. Just like you, I bought every gadget imaginable. When I could have skipped all those useless tools, and purchased the amazing Swiss Army Knife."

"We'll Google Swiss Army Knives tomorrow, and see if they're looking for a new spokesman. I need to go work on my history assignment." I bit my lip. "Stanley Preston is threatening me."

"Stanley's a bottom-feeder who's a necessary evil for you

to endure while attending Preston," Dad said. "Try and stay on his good side. Sophie's gone, and she's much better at dealing with that tool than I ever will be."

Wow, hell had frozen over because I think he got it. "So, I'm going to go, and we'll finish this gift giving thing tomorrow." I stood up.

"Park it."

I did. "If I don't get my history thing done, you get to tell Stanley Preston why," I said. "I do not want to lose my grades, my scholarship, or screw up college applications."

"Stanley Preston and his teeth scare me, sweetie. Besides it's Friday. You have the entire weekend to do Piranha Man's homework. Sophie and I debated whether it was the right time to give this to you. Your mama wanted you to have this when you turned eighteen."

He pulled something rectangular and bulky, covered in silks and other exotic fabrics out from under the desk, and cradled it. "You were born a month premature."

I knew this story. I'd heard it a hundred times. It was like the retelling of Mary and Joseph's trip to Bethlehem. "I know, Dad."

"Your mama was on bed rest for months, but that didn't stop you from entering this world when you wanted to. I held you in the palm of my hand. You were tiny, and so beautiful that I was almost scared you were not of this world." He looked up at the ceiling and blinked back some tears. "My allergies, again. This room is so dusty."

I offered him a napkin, but he wouldn't take it, and wiped his eyes with his hand. I stared at my gift. It was wrapped in crimson, purple, gold, and silver fabrics.

"I didn't think you were ready for this, but Sophie said you needed it now. So you decide, Maddie. Give me your gut answer. You're good when you go with your gut." He held this mysterious object in front of me. "Yes, or no?"

There were words painted on the fabrics. Some I recognized, but most were in different languages. Now I was more curious than tired. "I'm ready." I held out my arms toward him, toward my present.

"Ta-da!" He gingerly placed the gift into my arms.

I placed it on my lap. The fabrics covering my present were amazing. Some of the silks were smooth as ice, others rough to the touch. Some of the cottons were fuzzy like they'd just been picked from a bush. What languages were all these words written in? French, Italian, Aramaic?

"It's so pretty. I almost hate to…" Suddenly I felt like an archeologist who wanted to explore the outside, before discovering the inside of a mysterious site. But I couldn't wait one second longer, and started to unwind the fabrics and tossed them to the side.

"Careful, Maddie," Dad said. "Your mama collected those textiles from all over the globe: different artists as well as time periods. They're most likely priceless at this point, and worth more than your present, so don't discard them. You can make some cash selling them on eBay someday."

The present sat half unwrapped in my lap, the fabrics spilling toward the floor. I could see something underneath with pictures, foreign words, painted symbols and decoupage photos. I tried my best to carefully unwrap the rest of the cloth. And revealed a big, beautiful, handmade, leather-bound scrapbook.

It was thick. I opened the cover. The pages didn't lie flat. I turned them carefully. They were filled with memorabilia, trinkets, and notations in English, as well as foreign languages. *What was this?* It was wild.

"Your mama worked on that book for years—even before you were born. It was her obsession," Dad said. "When we looked for houses to buy, she had a couple of non-nego-tiables: one, a decent neighborhood not too far from Preston

Academy; two, a small room with windows and plenty of light in her study so she could finish her project. It's the history of your people from Rebecca's side of our family. What do you think? It's amazing, isn't it?"

I sat on the floor of Mama's study with this beautiful book on my lap. I knew I was supposed to feel joy. Pride. Family love. But I still felt heartsick, and a little angry.

"I feel… I feel lucky. So lucky that—" I pushed myself to standing, cradling my present. "I'm going to go check out the best present in the world, in my room. Thanks, Dad." I stretched up on my tiptoes and kissed him on the cheek.

I sat in my bed with the covers pulled up to my chin, and paged through the book. This is what Mama had been working on before she disappeared. This is what the huge white boards were for, the hours on the computer, all the hand written pages. This was the puzzle she was working on when I was still her puzzle piece.

I had already flipped through it, but now turned back and examined the first page. Mama had penned in her perfect cursive and underlined our immediate family's names. She had clipped snippets of family photos and glued them next to her recent entries. A cheesy, photo booth picture of her and Dad when they were in their twenties, and probably on a date. Me at age four wearing a ballerina tutu, smiling, arms overhead. Dad, when he was younger, looking over his shoulder, love burning through his eyes most likely directed at Mama, who took the photo. Finally, Dad's parents standing in front of their farmhouse in Wisconsin.

And all those notes and words. I'd have to spend some time trying to figure out what languages they were written in, as well as what they said.

31

Unlike other ancestry charts—which I had seen online and in TV shows—Mama's book was different. She included tiny pieces of memorabilia scattered throughout the lineage charts, outlined in the book. There were pieces of dried plants, tombstone etchings, old photographs, pressed flowers, pictures of jewelry, snippets of newspaper articles, even a bead and tiny crystals glued onto a page.

There were links to newspaper articles, and websites that were ten-plus-years-old, and might not even exist anymore. She must have spent hundreds of hours on this book that would only mean something to people in our family. I was exhausted, but had to check out just a few more pages. I laid my head back on my pillow and propped the book on my knees.

The nightmares always started the same way: I smelled burnt sage, lavender, and freshly baked chocolate chip cookies. Mama hunched over the steering wheel of our small car, sprigs of lavender and dried sage hanging next to her from the rearview mirror. She drove up a ramp through a garage with a low, claustrophobic ceiling.

There was no outer wall to the garage: just a skinny, metal chain that separated the concrete ramp from the air, and whatever existed beyond that. I was a tiny kid, and so was still strapped in a booster seat in the back of our clunker, munching on a cookie while driving in circles up this garage.

Suddenly, we accelerated like crazy, and I was sucked back into that seat while we sped up an endless, spiral ramp past parked cars. I wanted to be in one of those parked cars, 'cause I was getting dizzy and felt scared.

"Mama, slow down!" I said.

I saw her in the rearview mirror, her eyebrows pinched

together. Then she smiled at me for a heartbeat, and her brows relaxed. She put one hand to her mouth, and threw me a kiss. "Life goes fast, Madeline. Right now we need to be just like life. *We need to go very, very fast.*"

Tires squealed. Something strong and powerful slammed into our car from behind. Our tin can on wheels jolted and we were hit again. I heard a loud metal-on-metal BANG!

———

I woke up, startled. This was the first time I'd remembered that moment—probably because I visited the scene. I clutched her book to my chest. I wondered if there was a mistake, or a miracle, and maybe she could still be alive. A few tears leaked out, but I wiped them away.

I tossed and turned in the black of night while memories of her flooded my brain. Until I told myself, *enough,* and looked up at the iridescent, nighttime stars that Dad had painted on my ceiling. I frowned. "Thank you for my beautiful book, Mama. But you shouldn't have left. I will never forgive you for leaving," I whispered, closed my eyes, and eventually fell asleep.

CHAPTER 5

"*N*ow, you're beyond hot," Chaka said as she leaned back away from my face, holding a plump, blush brush in one hand.

It was the next day. I looked at my reflection in the huge, brightly lit bathroom mirror at Chaka's parents' zillionaire condo in One Mag Mile. I was dressed in a miniskirt with leggings, and wore skinny leather above-the-knee boots with sky-high heels. My top was an expensive skanky thing that sunk low on my chest and barely covered my butt. Hookerville, here I come.

"I know you're trying to cheer me up, but I don't think this makeover works for me," I said.

Aaron thrust a black, leather bomber jacket at me. "Put this on," he said. "It completes your bad girl look."

"I look like a cross between Amanda Seyfried, Amanda Knox, who I always believed was innocent, and a Miley Cyrus transvestite," I said. "I want to go home."

"Not until you have some fun." Chaka squeezed my arm. "My dad's friend is having an invite-only party for his new art exhibit. His sons are smokin'. They're twins, seniors at Latin School. I bet they'll be there."

I shook my head. "I'm not feeling the party vibe."

"Hot twins and an art exhibit?" Aaron said. "Oh yes, you are."

"This is the best idea I've had in weeks." Chaka rubbed her hands together.

Twenty minutes later, Aaron, Chaka, and I were on the L train platform waiting on the train to go to a private party that probably had cute, smart guys that might change my mood from rotten to okay. I never rode the train; I hated it. The bus with its creepy overpass was bad enough.

The L platforms towered high above the streets. They were completely fenced in so supposedly, you couldn't fall off them down onto the sidewalks and onto the streets below. There were people of all ages and attires waiting to go somewhere. A few peered into the distance looking for their trains. Some sat calmly on the skinny benches under the thin, ugly, metal overhangs.

Chaka wore D&G and looked stylish, as always. Aaron hadn't changed clothes, just jacked upped his attitude. That seemed to work for him.

I teetered on the too-tall boots, and smelled something sweet that I realized was the makeup slathered on my face. I blinked and tried to see past the false eyelashes Chaka had glued on my lids. There was no way this would be my new, standard, party look.

A bunch of gang kids with tats, ratty clothes, and too many piercings bolted up the stairs to the platform, punching each other, swearing, talking trash, and laughing. I covered my ears with my hands.

I didn't make eye contact with them, but walked away toward the tracks. Other commuters did the same. Chaka and Aaron were debating something, and didn't even register that I had slipped through the crowd, until I was fifteen feet down the platform.

Two of the gang kids—a girl and a guy—started screaming at each other. A third kid, a tall guy pulled a knife and told them to knock it off, and save it for home turf.

I looked around and saw three suits hitting 911 on their cells. The L train roared toward our station. Jeez, what had I gotten myself into? I should have just gone home.

"Hey, it's you isn't it? Dressed a little differently, but it's still you," an older guy said. "I think I'd recognize you anywhere."

I spotted a glimpse of a man wearing a leather bomber jacket slipping away through the crowds. Right then, the gang dispute moved toward me, and suddenly, I was in the middle of it.

"Oh, is she your biyatch, now?" A gang girl with spiked hair said and knuckle-jabbed me in the arm.

"I don't even know him." I tried to back away. But someone yanked me from behind, and stopped me.

The gang guy fighting with the girl leered at me, "She's a finer piece than you." He ran his finger across my cheek.

My heart raced, and I felt my throat starting to close off. Please no, not another panic attack. Not two in two days.

Chaka noticed. "Madeline! Just walk away from them." She pushed her way through the crowd toward me. "You leave her alone!"

I tried to step away. But I felt a hard shove in my ribs, which catapulted me sideways. I toppled off the L platform, and dropped toward the train tracks that lay yards below. I had no air in my lungs to scream but others did.

Through the chaos I heard a woman whisper, "*Madeline.*"

She sounded so calm and familiar. But that didn't matter when my butt hit the gravel next to the concrete wall and a shock of pain blasted up my spine. I felt a pop behind my right shoulder blade, and it took my breath away.

The woman said, "*Madeline. Come to me.*" Her message was drowned out by the screech from the oncoming train.

I lay on the gravel next to the tracks, as voices and sounds swirled around me. Time slowed down like freeze frames in a download that wasn't tracking properly. This was nothing like my accident when I was six-years-old, and I blacked out.

I was wide awake, heard a piercing whistle, and knew a train was approaching. I tried to swivel my neck to see how far away it was. Not a good idea. My neck and back muscles spasmed something awful, and fiery sensations shot through my back, arms, and legs. My body locked, and I couldn't really move; I felt like I was caught within a cage. Out of the corner of my eyes I spotted the L train blasting down the tracks, headed straight toward me.

Guess everyone had a time to die. Since I'd skipped death ten years ago, this was most likely my time. Maybe getting run over by a train wouldn't hurt that much, if I was already numb from my fall. Maybe, I should pray for that to happen. So, I did. That's when everything shot to black.

CHAPTER 6

I woke up feeling like death on toast. My head felt like someone had stuck a hundred tiny knives into my brain. Every inch of my body ached, and my eyelids were heavy—like they had been glued shut. I probably had the worst flu imaginable.

I was on my stomach, lying on something rough and scratchy. I bet Dad had tucked me into bed with one of his favorite Mexican artisan woolen blankets. I loved the beauty of the patterns, as well as the devotion and care that went into their craftsmanship. But, I was allergic to wool, and they made me itch—which Dad always forgot.

I wiggled my fingers, and opened my eyes: everything was blurry. A chicken high-stepped in front of me, and we made eye contact. Odd. First, 'cause I haven't had a meaningful moment with a chicken unless it was seasoned with herbs de Provence', baked and sitting next to some steamed vegetables on a plate in front of me. Second, because the hen and I were on the same level, both lying on an outdoor dirt ground interrupted with chewed-up pieces of grass. Well, I was lying, but the hen was walking.

The chicken stared at me, blinked and clucked like a worried mom. She apparently had other pressing concerns to attend to, so she abandoned me and strutted past more people scattered on the ground.

One was a thin, young woman collapsed on her stomach. A long skirt was bunched up over her knees, and her legs were covered in weird, white, puffy leggings. She wore a long-sleeved shirt, and a little white cap shoved onto one side of her head. White cap?

I shut my eyes, exhausted. I couldn't place this woman. I'd never seen her at school, or in any neighborhood I'd been in. Maybe she was a dream or a delusion. Possibly a character in an old movie I'd been watching before I fell asleep. I blinked, opened my eyes and the woman with the white cap was still in my peripheral vision. I turned my head toward her, and my vision focused.

Her pretty face was twisted at an odd angle, and her eyes stared frozen into mine. Her shirt buttoned all the way to her throat was caked in dark red, drying blood, probably due to the fact that her neck was nearly severed. She was dead.

I hyperventilated, and my stomach heaved. I rolled onto my side, and vomited. I felt so embarrassed and wiped my mouth. I pushed myself up to my elbows, glanced around and spotted more people, probably close to ten total—children, adults—all dressed in similar, strange outfits lying twisted and torqued on the ground close by me. *Where was I?*

Most of the men were dead with gaping holes in their chests. Several women and children looked like they were stabbed with knives or hatchets. An older guy even had crispy, burnt pants and sleeves. I caught a glimpse of his arm. It was red and blistered. He didn't care because he wasn't breathing. They all were broken, bloody, and definitely dead.

I pushed myself to sitting, and winced in pain as my head throbbed. Something white and red hung in front of my eyes.

I pulled the annoying thing off—it was a small, white cap covered in blood, just like the cap on the woman with the severed neck.

But this was *my* bloody cap. Bile rose in my throat. I gagged, and flung it as far away from me as possible.

I've had lots of nightmares in my life. Dreams of the car chase that led up to the car accident where Mama disappeared, and funky, psychedelic dreams about those stained glass skylights at Preston Academy. The dreams didn't usually make any sense, but this one had to be one of the worst ever: this dream felt so *real*.

The broken earth rubbed against my skin, and penetrated my pores. The leaves and grass underneath my body were scratchy. The smell of burning wood made my nose twitch. I sneezed and coughed.

I jammed my hands down the sides of my body searching for my anti-anxiety drugs, but couldn't find the bottle. What happened to my pockets? I had no pockets. I hyperventilated and tried to remember to breathe slow and relaxed, like in yoga: calm, deep breaths in, soothing, deep breaths out. That's when I spotted the fiery remains of a small, rustic cabin squatted on a low hill in the near distance. I started shaking.

Flames flared through this tiny, wooden structure. Embers floated up into the air like fireflies twinkling just above my head at my grandparents' place in the Wisconsin countryside during a late, Indian summer. But I didn't think this was Wisconsin.

I pushed myself off the ground, and stumbled like a drunken person toward the cabin. Maybe I could help someone in there. Maybe someone could help me. "Hello?" I said. But nothing came out of my mouth, and no one answered me.

I wiped away a few tears, saw blood on my hands and

realized the cut on the right side of my head extended down into my forehead. It had bled through my hair and was seeping into my eye. "Is there anyone here?" I yelled. Again, apparently I was yelling to myself.

I put a hand to my mouth. My lips moved, but I couldn't talk. No sounds came out of my mouth. Why? What the hell was wrong with me?

There was a dark, dense forest about twenty yards from the rear of the torched, smoldering cabin. I squinted through the smoky air, and wiped my eyes. Where was I? Was I back at the Chicago Neurological Foundation where they tried to diagnose my anxiety after Mama disappeared? Was I heavily medicated on major anti-psychotics, and institutionalized someplace with locked doors, gates, and guards? Had I finally lost it for good?

I closed my eyes, and sat back on the ground. Maybe if I took a moment to center and calm myself, this crazy show playing in my head would disappear. I visualized myself tucked into bed, looking up at my ceiling at the glow stars and iridescent maps of the world that Dad had painted up there for me to look at when I couldn't sleep. After a few moments, I felt calmer and opened my eyes.

The same dead people lay on the ground and the cabin continued to simmer. A frustrated cry escaped my lips, and I wiped my tears away with my bloodstained, muddied, long sleeve. Then I realized—I had a voice. It was bare bones basic, but it was a voice.

In the distance I heard a worried, adult female shout, "Abigail?"

I didn't know who Abigail was, but I'd *love* to see a friendly person right about now. "Yes!" I said, but couldn't quite get the word out of my mouth. Like, I still didn't know how to work this mouth, this voice.

"Abigail, we are coming for thee!" the woman said. Whoever she was couldn't get here soon enough.

That's when I first saw him.

He looked about my age, with strong cheekbones and black, shiny hair that swept onto his shoulders. He wore a long, tanned, animal hide shirt and loose pants. He was tall, muscular, stunning. He also looked very much alive. *I really liked the alive part.*

He and another big, built, young man skirted the remains of the torched cabin and headed toward the forest. The other guy also had black hair, but his skin was caramel, and he wore old-fashioned pilgrim breeches and a plain shirt. They carried bows and arrows. The one clutched a knife. They both looked hard and tough like rebels or even the punks on the el platform.

The young man with the strong cheekbones scanned the scene. His gaze was intense, especially when it landed on me. His hazel eyes regarded me with coldness, disdain. I had no idea why. He looked dangerous, but not like a killer. There was something different about him that I couldn't explain. He nodded at me once, turned, and followed the other guy into the forest.

And left me with all the dead people.

Except for the woman who kept calling for Abigail. I spotted her. She was pretty, young, and accompanied by two men, one older and one younger. They were dressed in strange, colonial attire, and crouched low to the ground as they crept up the hill toward the cabin and me.

The woman paused next to a body of a girl lying on her stomach. The woman bit her lip so hard I thought she'd draw blood. "Abigail?" she asked.

The older man kneeled in the dirt, and turned the girl's body over. "She's dead, Mistress. They're all dead," he said.

The woman grimaced, leaned over, and smoothed back

the blood-caked hair that covered the dead girl's face. She looked relieved, then embarrassed. "'Tis not Abigail." She gently shut the dead girl's eyes with her hand. "Go to God."

"Mistress Elizabeth." The older man pushed himself back to standing. "I pray that your cousin is alive. But you are in grave danger here. Daniel will escort you back to the garrison. I will look for Abigail."

Elizabeth jutted her chin out, determined. "Most of our men are days' journey away fighting this war. I am not a foolish woman, and do not for one second believe we are that much safer at the garrison, either." She stood up incredibly tall and stared down the man who challenged her.

"But we are in the middle of a war, as these bodies and burnt buildings attest to." He gestured broadly. "I swore an oath to King Charles II, whom I have never met, to fight this war and protect this land. I promised your husband, General Jebediah Ballard, whom I have fought next to in battle, dined with and respect deeply, that I would keep you, his wife, safe from harm."

"Abigail is my cousin," Elizabeth said. "Dead or alive, I will find her. Only then will I return to the garrison." She scrutinized the area. "Abigail?" she hollered.

Elizabeth looked so nice, so sweet, and I really needed a friend. Even if this was only a dream, I wanted a friend. So I made a decision.

"Yes," I said and the word came out of my mouth garbled. I lifted my arm off the dirt, high up in the air to get Elizabeth's attention. But she was already turning in my direction.

Her hand clasped her chest and she froze for a second. And melted just as quickly. "Abigail!" Elizabeth raced toward me, maneuvering around dead bodies, singed grass, smoldering bales of hay, a small, wooden wagon that was tipped over on its side. "Abigail!" She skidded to a stop, and awkwardly fell onto her knees next to me.

43

"It is a miracle you are alive!" She burst into tears, and threw her arms around me. "I knew it. I felt it in my soul. God wouldn't let you die. You had to be here." She hugged me tight.

Her embrace filled me with joy, but practically killed my back and my ribs. I winced.

Elizabeth understood and released me slowly back to the earth. She frowned and fussed over me. "Your head is bleeding. I need to see your wound." She smoothed my bloody hair back from my forehead. "It is deep, but I believe if we use the doctor's medicine, it will heal just right," she said. "Where else do you have pain?"

I tried to shrug my shoulders, but that hurt too, so I stopped. "I'm okay, I think." I didn't tell Elizabeth that this moment only existed in my dream; that the next minute we might be wearing tutus, eating cupcakes at some cute bakery, and dishing about guys. This definitely wasn't the time to tell her that.

Elizabeth's male guardians arrived and stared at me, relieved but worried.

"William." Elizabeth pointed at the older man. "Give Abigail water." He did. Elizabeth propped me up, as I sipped from a small metal cup. "When I heard the rumors that Philip's warriors attacked the Endicott settlement, I went mad with worry," she said. "Dearest cousin, I prayed you were alive." She blinked, and wiped her eyes with the back of her hand. "My prayers are answered because here you are, Abigail. You are the only one alive. God has plans for you."

Even though this was a terrible nightmare, Elizabeth was kind.

"Thank you for rescuing me," I said and stopped talking, because even I heard those words exit my mouth. They were quiet words, but sounded normal. At least I wasn't some daft mute in this dream.

"I'm really sorry, but…" I put my hand to my head where it throbbed like crazy. "I'm not sure where I am."

"You have been through a distressing ordeal. I cannot imagine what you have seen." She motioned to the young man behind her. "Daniel hand me the medicinals." He gave her a flask.

She leaned back toward me with the tin cup re-filled with water. "Drink this. You are safe for now," she said. "But we need to leave here quickly."

I glanced around; saw all the dead, twisted bodies and the burning cabin. I looked up into the sky that had puffs of smoke and birds flying through them cawing to each other, like old friends saying hello. How could all these birds be so calm during this bloodbath?

I started shaking again. "Where am I?"

"All will be fine." She held the cup next to my lips. "Drink."

I did. Almost immediately I felt relaxed, calmer. I wondered where all those birds were going, and I remembered the beautiful, young man dressed in animal skins, with long black hair that curled around his shoulders.

My body felt tingly, my brain a little fuzzy. I swear I saw Mama standing behind Elizabeth. She regarded me with a flash of excitement in her clear eyes. She held up something small that was overall dull, but still had a hint of a sparkle. I couldn't make out what it was.

But Mama was so excited and said, "Look Madeline! It's an important piece of our puzzle. I think I found the place where this puzzle piece fits just perfectly." She laughed and grabbed my six-year-old hands. We giggled and twirled in circles in the center of a green, grassy field filled with wild flowers.

CHAPTER 7

*W*hen I woke, Mama was gone. I was lying on some kind of mat on a wooden floor next to a big, stone fireplace in a dark room lit only by fat, drippy candles. There were logs stacked in bundles nearby, leaning against a rough wall.

I was covered in blankets and sweating buckets. A thick, cloth bandage covered the gash on my forehead and poked down toward my right eye.

I blinked, wiggled my hand out from the cocoon of blankets, snagged the annoying bandage, and pushed it away so I could see more clearly—another whacked dream?

"Abigail. You are awake." Elizabeth, my savior, leaned over and regarded me, worried.

Nah, this wasn't another dream, just a continuation of my previous nightmare.

She placed one finger firmly on my bandage. "Do not fuss with your dressing," she said. "You have a deep cut and a hard blow to your skull. Doctor Thorpe is away, and we had to dress your wound the best we knew how."

"Thank you." I could barely get the words out, as my

mouth felt like I'd been chewing sand. "Could I have something to drink, please?" Maybe electrolyte water and a juice smoothie followed with a double shot of mocha espresso, as I'd love a little energy right now.

She nodded and reached behind her. "Doctor Thorpe accompanies our brave men and the other troops, as the war has moved down the coast, as well as inland." She bit her lip.

Apparently my ongoing nightmare included me being injured in a war. (*Note to self: turn off The History Channel an hour before going to bed.*)

"We are short-handed, but we will make do. Sit up. You are sweating out your wound, and you need to drink."

I nodded, propped my free hand behind me and tried to push myself to a seated position. She put her arm around my shoulders, helped lift me to sitting and put a metallic cup to my lips. I downed the cool water in seconds.

"You must be starving." She stuck a bowl of what looked and smelled like cheap, canned, dog food in front of me. "Eat."

My nose crinkled and I shook my head. "No. I can't eat that."

She frowned, but placed the bowl behind her. "Very well. You will eat when you are hungry. When Tobias told us about the attack, everyone prayed for your immortal soul. But only Angeni took my hand and made me visualize you, alive, healthy and happy in this life. She told me I must go and find you." Elizabeth poured me another cup of water.

"Mmm." I gulped it and emptied the cup. "More?"

She shook her head and took the cup away. "No, everything in moderation. Now you must rest." She pressed the bandage firmly on my head. I winced. "No fidgeting. You need to heal."

Healing sounded great. What sounded even better would be waking up in my bed, feeling the rumble of the L train

PAMELA DUMOND

clattering down the street outside my bedroom window and hearing my dad holler, "Rise and shine, girls!" I needed to be at home. Not wherever this dream had taken me.

So I decided to use the trick I reserved for the times my dreams got too bizarre: *I chose to wake up now.* The quickest way to do this was to thank the key players in my dream to their face. I'd wish them my very best and say goodbye. Then, voilà! I'd wake up to my real nightmare, which was my actual life in Chicago.

"Elizabeth," I clasped this woman's hand with my free hand, and gazed up at her.

"Yes, Abigail." She smiled. "I swear your hand feels cooler already. You are healing, I know it."

This woman was far too helpful and kind, which was not helping me get rid of her. "Thank you for rescuing me, Elizabeth. You put yourself in danger. You were brave and strong," I said. "I can't repay you, but I'll always remember you." Bit of a lie; I usually didn't remember the people in my dreams. But it sounded more polite, which was a nice way to say goodbye to imaginary people.

"That is a lovely sentiment. Now lay back down." She helped lower me to the mat on the floor. I lay flat, as she tucked me in tightly with the blankets next to the warm fireplace. The gash on my forehead burned like angry wasps had stung it.

This was the perfect time to go back to my real life. I was already sleepy. My eyelids started to close when that beautiful young man's face popped into my brain, and startled me. He was like a puzzle piece. I wanted to know more about him. Did he fit in my life?

No! I was having a ridiculous fantasy, and it was time for this dream to end. I bit my lip. "I have to be honest with you."

"Tomorrow. The medicinals in your water will help you

sleep soundly," she replied. "May your dreams be pious. I expect to see you nearly recovered by the morning."

Medicinals? Was she drugging me? Is that why I felt so woozy? These feelings didn't fit a normal, dream sequence. Usually I could break out of a dream quickly. But here I felt slow—like I was trying to jog through mud. But, I had to say it.

"Elizabeth?"

"Yes, Abigail."

"Stop calling me Abigail. My name is Madeline Blackford. I've never met you before today, and I don't have a clue who you are."

Her eyebrows pinched together. "You have been through an ordeal." Elizabeth patted my shoulder. "Sweet dreams, Abigail," she said and walked away.

CHAPTER 8

I woke, opened my eyes and blasts of sunshine poked through skinny clouds in blue skies overhead. Nightmare over, mission accomplished! It looked like a decent fall day in Chicago streaming through my bedroom skylight before the weather got awful. Bonus: it was the weekend.

I'd hit a yoga class with Chaka. Maybe afterwards we'd grab Aaron and drop by some gallery openings in River North. Yummy. That's when I heard a horse whinny, and saw a chubby guy dressed in baggy capris lead that horse past me.

This was not good. "Help!" I said. The chubby guy didn't even look up. The horse turned and looked me square in the eyes. I flinched, lifted my head, and realized I was being carried down a skinny, dirt path on a rickety stretcher.

They lugged me past a line of decrepit, tiny, wooden buildings in a hick settlement worse than any *Little House on the Prairie* cable re-run I'd ever seen.

"Oh, for God's sake," I said. "Will this flippin' dream never end?"

Elizabeth walked next to my stretcher, her lips pursed

like she was an angry version of Mary Poppins. That is if Mary were seven months pregnant. Funny I hadn't noticed that 'til now.

Now, I noticed everything. Elizabeth's hair was pulled back in a severe bun, and the top of her head was covered with one of those white, doily cloths. Her face flushed, and she peered at me, irritated. She leaned her face right next to mine—like she meant to be friendly. But instead she pinched my cheek.

"Just because you hit your head on a stone in the middle of a vicious attack, Abigail, does not mean you can take God's name in vain," she said. "I am taking you to the Reverend Wilkins. He is an educated man, very sensible. Perhaps he can determine what is wrong with your memory. At least we can pray for you. Maybe then we can make everything right."

"Nice try, Elizabeth. But the fact that I'm still here means everything isn't right," I said. She frowned more but held her head high and kept on walking. Why was I still here? I had a hundred percent success rate of leaving bad dreams when I followed my oh-so-polite formula—until now.

My forehead pulsed, and I rubbed it. The lumpy bandage was still stuck on it, but at least my head didn't hurt quite as badly. Obviously, Elizabeth wasn't going to give up and vanish, or turn into a frog like my recurring dream. The one with the airline attendant who told me my luggage weighed far too much, and I'd have to pay extra to get on the flight.

I scoped my surroundings and eyed the guy who carried the lower part of my stretcher. He was one of the guys who rescued me, and he looked like the weak link.

He was short, scruffy, and probably in his twenties. I wrestled the blanket half off me and sat up. The stretcher wobbled, and I struggled to brace myself while I glared at him. "You are totally kidnapping me," I said. "Put me down. Immediately."

His eyes grew huge. "Yes, Miss Abigail." He lowered his end of the stretcher toward the ground.

Elizabeth stared daggers at him. "Daniel Winters, you swore allegiance to King Charles II, and promised my husband under oath that you would help me while he was gone fighting this war," she said. "Do not let this stretcher rest on the ground, not even for one second, until we have reached our destination."

Daniel's eyes widened and he jacked my stretcher back up into the air, which made me fall backwards. "Ow!" I exclaimed, and thought about Aaron with his flair for drama.

It wasn't easy, but with some effort I sat back up and pointed my index finger at Daniel like a magician, or a witch. "Daniel Winters," I said. "I am not from your world. I have magical powers that will… strike you. Give you stink eye, or hand rot or… or… make your manhood shrivel."

Guess that got his attention, 'cause his forehead broke out in a sweat and he peered down at his pants.

"Lower me to the ground *now*!"

He mumbled, but lowered my stretcher. I was only a foot from the dirt ground, which probably wouldn't be a height issue for me. I was seconds from freedom, but only if I had the nerve to break out of here.

That's when a guy close to my head stifled a laugh. "Be very frightened, Daniel. Because Miss Abigail who dreams of fancy, English gowns, bonnets, and meeting King Charles II some day, has suddenly become a warrior. And she threatened not only you," he said, "but I do believe your future offspring, as well."

This smart mouthed commentary came from near my head and I twisted, turned and tried to see the jerk, but was trapped and stifled by all the blankets. "Don't think for one second, dude, that you're safe from my magic powers, either."

He snorted in laughter again. "Now I am as frightened of you as I am of King Philip and his warriors."

"Who?" I floundered but just seemed to get more tangled in the blankets. The only thing I gained from my efforts was frustration.

"Shush, Samuel. You of all people should know better." Elizabeth pinched Daniel's arm. "I will not hide your poor judgment, or let you go unpunished should you choose to disobey orders, Daniel. You will be charged with disorderly conduct, your military record will be permanently scarred. And you might find yourself facing time in the stocks."

Daniel looked at Elizabeth wide-eyed. Then the wuss hoisted his end back up in the air, and continued carrying me wherever this journey led.

Elizabeth marched calmly next to me, and patted her blossoming belly. I no longer liked her for rescuing me. Right now I actually disliked her. Intensely.

"No!" I slammed my hand against the cot. "No! I told you I am *not* Abigail. I do not belong here. I want to go home. Now!"

Daniel shuddered. Elizabeth didn't flinch, let alone bat an eye. The guy above my head carrying the front handles cleared his throat.

I looked down at the ground. Yes, the drop was higher than before, but it was still only three or four feet. If I jumped or rolled off, maybe I'd only suffer a few bruises. It wouldn't be like dangling off a ten-story, parking garage, hovering between earth and sky. Suffering amnesia as well as anxiety.

If I landed in one piece, nothing badly broken, I'd bolt. I'd run so far away from Elizabeth and her crew, and hopefully stumble on a safe, hiding place where they couldn't easily find me. I'd find the right words to say that would break this nightmare, and bring me back to my life in Chicago. But then I saw something so creepy it made me second guess my plans.

They lugged me through a part of this hellhole that was a pathetic, tiny, central park or village commons. There was a small, but sturdy, wood building. Next to it was torture devices I'd only seen in history books: stocks to publicly humiliate and punish people.

A worried-looking, wrinkled, middle-aged guy with huge round eyes was imprisoned in one of them, seated on a bench, his hands locked into a contraption that didn't allow him to move them. A sign crudely scrawled underneath him said, "LIAR."

The guy caught my eye. "I am not a liar, Miss Abigail. Do you believe me?" I didn't know what to say to him. I didn't even know who he was. So, I just nodded.

Next to the guy in the stocks was a whipping post. Close to that was a hanging platform. *No, no.* Give me Taylor and her bitchy friends at Preston Academy any day, 'cause I definitely didn't belong here. Bye-bye. It was past time that I left this bizarre place. I closed my eyes, crossed my fingers, pushed myself off the cot, and landed with a thump on my butt on the ground.

CHAPTER 9

*T*angled in the stupid blankets, I fumbled around for seconds, like a kid thrown into the pool who didn't know how to swim.

Daniel said, "I did not do that." He whistled nervously.

Elizabeth frowned. "Abigail, you are making a mistake." She leaned down to grab me, or help me. I wasn't sure, but it didn't matter at this point—because I was done.

I tore off the blankets, pushed myself to standing and ran. Where to head? I didn't have a clue.

I sprinted past women in long, puffy, drab skirts chatting with each other, as they held freshly killed, bloody chickens upside down, while they absent-mindedly plucked the feathers from their scrawny, still-twitching bodies.

I dodged around defeated-looking, hunched over colonial soldiers carrying beat-up weapons and wearing dirty, ragged clothes.

I whipped my head over my shoulder to see if I was being pursued. Dang! That simple movement shot pain up from my ribs through my neck and into the slash above my eye. Daniel careened after me like a colonial Frankenstein.

I slammed into somebody, and caught myself on his skinny, long, black-sleeved arms.

"Oof!" he exclaimed. His very, long face was surrounded by greasy, silver hair. He was rail-thin, freakishly tall and dressed in a black suit of sorts. He wore what looked like a permanent scowl and clutched a fat Bible.

"Miss Abigail?" he squeaked and clutched his stomach.

"Sorry, sir!" I pushed away from him, and kept on running. My head pulsed, I felt dizzy and out of breath. What happened to my healthy swimmer's lungs where I could do lap after lap and just be a little winded? Before I landed in this weird dream I was completely in shape. Now I couldn't even escape through some rural, nightmare town without being completely exhausted. *(Note to self: delusion. Not real. Get a grip.)*

I spotted a rustic, tiny, thatched hut, which looked like— no—it *felt* like the perfect place to hide behind, and regroup. I rounded its corner, and collapsed on my knees onto the ground next to it. The shack was made of tree branches woven together. A thick layer of intertwined skinny branches and braided leaves comprised its roof.

I hid behind the hut, clasped my hand over my mouth, and tried to cover my loud, labored breathing. I had to be quiet, or Elizabeth and her crew would catch me. I peeked out from around the hut's edge. Daniel lumbered away in the opposite direction from my hiding spot. The tall, skinny guy shook the Bible in Elizabeth's face, while he complained and lectured her half to death.

To her credit she listened and nodded. But Elizabeth was no one's fool. She glanced around the entire time, most likely looking for me. But it seemed like I was safe for a moment tucked away behind my new refuge.

Unlike the other drab, brown buildings in this eyesore of a village, this hut had some fading flowers and herbs planted in the ground around it. I touched the ground next to the herbs, and felt a calming sensation in my throat and chest. It made me think the person who planted them had a way not only with green, living things, but perhaps knew how to soothe anxious people as well. I relaxed, closed my eyes and imagined my dad, Sophie, and even Jane back in Chicago.

When somebody tall and strong wrapped a muscular arm around my shoulders from behind, pulled me backward and pinned me firmly to his chest. I tried to scream, but he covered my mouth with his calloused hand and whispered into my ear, "If you shout they will find you. Despite our differences, I would never hurt you, Abigail."

I recognized my captor's voice. He was the guy who carried the top end of the stretcher—the guy who laughed at me. "Let me go," I mumbled.

"If you yell they will find you in seconds," he said.

"Got it." This guy pissed me off, but he was right.

"Finally we agree on something. Now that is a miracle." He released his hand from my mouth. But his strong arm still wrapped around my upper chest, and anchored me to him.

Elizabeth excused herself from the Reverend and waddled to Daniel's side. "You must find her," she said. "Abigail is a danger to herself."

"Are you?" the guy asked me.

"Yes," I whispered. "I'm in danger of my sister eating my share of Dad's homemade, breakfast frittata if I oversleep. Then I'll get stuck with the seaweed energy bar. Which is not only dangerous—but scary, too."

"I do not—" he said.

"Right. You don't get it. You don't understand. Because whoever you are, in wherever I'm at? You're incredibly rude and downright mean to make fun of my situation." I tried to squirm from his grasp. But his arm was like a vise and I couldn't break free. "What is wrong with you?" I asked, beyond frustrated.

"What is wrong with me?" he asked. "You were the only person rescued after a vicious attack by King Philip's warriors on the Endicott settlement. Everyone in that outpost died horrible, bloody deaths, except for you. Your friends and family traveled for hours, and risked their own lives with the smallest hopes that they would find you still breathing."

"You don't understand."

"You are right. I do not. After your family and friends picked through the mutilated bodies and found you alive, they carried you back to the garrison, tended to your wounds and stayed awake for days to make sure you would survive your injuries and awaken on the living side of God's creation. Now you repay them with hostility and arrogance. Yet you ask what is wrong with me."

I felt a flash of anger and pride that burnt my cheeks and my neck. Then I felt shame, because in a way, this guy was right. If I put aside the absurdity of my situation, I could see that these characters in their odd clothes with their strange way of speaking *were* trying to help me. Perhaps if *they were real,* this guy would have a valid point.

But his very muscular arm clasped across me that prevented me from running away couldn't be real. And I wasn't about to let some guy in a nightmare make me feel any worse than I felt when I was awake in my real life.

I shook my head. "That's not true. What happened on that field with those dead people, what's happening right now, it's—"

"What?" he asked, his breath warm and moist against the skin of my neck.

I felt his firm grip across my chest loosen. "What's happening right now is not real."

Let him be angry with me. Let this entire crew of helpful, loving, creepy people wearing terrible outfits, living in a totally strange, imaginary world get pissed off at me. At least I was—for the most part—honest and told the truth.

"What do you mean?" he asked.

"I've been through this before. I went to psychotherapy for this. I must be crazy for even sharing this with you, but I will, because you are the guy who is *not* willing to let me go."

"I would be thrilled to let you go. However I promised Elizabeth I would help her."

"Head's up, dude. Elizabeth is an illusion. It's been confirmed by over five shrinks that whatever we're sharing right now, is either a nightmare, or delusion that my brain is creating." I felt his hair graze against my cheek. "And for the most part, I can't control these nightmares."

But, I had to admit the combination of his strong arms and warm breath on my skin felt a little hot. Fine. Apparently I was having a typical, teenage, *hormonal nightmare*.

"I have known you and Elizabeth since I was a boy. I spent enough time around here to know you are both flesh and blood. Although, I would not mind if she was real, and you were simply a nightmare," he said.

Excuse me? This guy was in my face about Abigail—why? "Listen to me," I said. "Apparently my brain tries to escape when I'm stressed. It creates fancy, imaginary situations and exotic people that are technically called delusions."

"My brain does not make delusions," he said.

Yeah, 'cause you're perfect. *Calm down, Madeline,* I told myself. *Getting angry with people in dreams never gets you anywhere.* "The docs think it's partially my heredity and my anxiety disorder thing." I wondered why I'd never had a prior delusion where any guy held me this tight. "So, basically, this whole thing isn't your fault, and you're off the hook."

"I know where I come from, I know whom I like and who

does not like me," he said. "I do this to help Elizabeth. Not you."

"Congrats. You're practically a boy scout. And lifetimes ahead of me in the good karma and mental health department."

"You complain that you are kidnapped," he said. "You insist this is a dream. But I tell you I have never dreamt of holding a woman, who did not want to be held."

I could feel in my gut that this guy was angry. He dropped his arm from my chest, and I felt him step away from me. My entire body swayed for a few seconds.

"I will not do this anymore, Abigail. I will not try and protect you," he said. "Even to help Elizabeth. You are free. Go and do whatever you wish."

I stopped wobbling, sucked in my core muscles, and stood up straight. "Thank you." I stretched my neck from side to side. "I don't need yours, or anyone else's protection. I'll wake up in an hour or even minutes and be back the next day at my school. Maybe I'll even Google this whole dream and see your face in a movie I watched, or a .com site I follow." I twisted my neck and managed to crack it. "Yes, that feels better."

"Google?" the guy asked.

Time to get out of here. But in order to leave my dream I still needed to thank him face to face. "Elizabeth called you Samuel. That's your name, right?" I turned and stared up into his face. And all the adrenaline that raged through my body abandoned me in one, long heartbeat.

Because the young man I had to say goodbye to, was the same beautiful guy with the hazel eyes and the long, black hair that curled around his shoulders. The guy who acknowledged me before he disappeared into the woods, while dead, mangled bodies lay behind him, littered in his path. Oh, no.

I felt dizzy and everything spun around me. I jammed the

palm of my hand onto my forehead, and winced as that tore into the gash on my head. "Oh thank you," I said to Samuel, who was not only a rebel, but quite possibly a killer. "Must go now." I stumbled away from him, completely freaked.

A short, older woman with a face etched with enough lines to fill a road map and an impossibly thick, long, silver braid of hair that hung down her back stepped out of the hut and nabbed my hand.

"Welcome, Abigail," she said. "I am so excited you are here. Would you like to come inside my home? You could tell me all about your dreams while I tend to your forehead."

I saw Elizabeth and Daniel pointing in different directions, not sure which way to hunt for me. Samuel glared. This woman's hand felt soothing just like the earth I touched next to this hut. "Okay," I said. "That sounds great." I let her lead me away but I felt Samuel's hazel eyes on me: confused, angry, and judgmental.

Apparently she did, too. "Thank you for your help, Samuel," she said. "It is time for you to leave."

He frowned and kicked the earth. A young man called out, "Samuel! Hurry up. Leave that poor, Abigail girl alone." Samuel glanced at the guy then back at me.

"Go. Have fun. But no matter what Tobias says—do not stay out with him after dark," the silver haired woman said, and led me inside her hut.

$\mathcal{T}$he inside of this tiny dwelling was proportioned like a field huddle of Chicago Bears' football players on game day: round, compact, and incredibly dense. Every inch of the dark space was packed. Drying plants hung from the ceiling. Fur pelts covered low benches. Rough metal and clay bowls and pots sat next to a small, open fire pit dug into the earth in the hut's center. There was actually a hole built into the roof above it, and smoke drifted out.

Oddly enough, this woman's home still looked and felt comfortable as well as friendly. Not like your neighborhood's crazy-hoarder-lady's place; more like your favorite great auntie who thought the stack of newspapers printed the day Diana married Prince Charles, as well as the newspapers on the day she died, might be valuable in the future. Which is why she saved them for you.

We sat next to each other on mats on the ground. She filled a small, sturdy, ceramic bowl with leaves and berries. "All the gossip-starved tongues in this garrison are wagging about you," she said and poured liquid from a flask into the bowl. "How lucky Abigail was to escape the massacre at the Endicott settlement."

She ground the concoction together with a pestle and mortar-like utensils. Then she handed the bowl to me along with the instruments. "Mix that for me, please."

I had never used a mortar and pestle before, but I did what she asked. Could it be all that different from stirring a bowl of cookie dough?

She stood, reached for some herbs hanging from the ceiling of her hut, pinched off some leaves and crumpled them between her fingers. "Show me," she said.

"Show you what?" I edged away from her, worried she'd turn into another weirdo from whatever dream I was in.

"The contents of that bowl, silly."

"Oh," I said, relieved, and held it out to her.

She dipped her index finger into it and swirled it around. She pulled out a dab and rubbed it on her wrist on top of a big jagged scar. She nodded. "Good." She sprinkled more pinches of this and that into the concoction. "More mixing please."

So I did.

"Do you remember the last time you were here?" she asked. "Answer truthfully."

"No." Why did she look so familiar? In all honestly, I didn't have a clue where I would know her—especially not as Abigail. "What's your name, Ma'am?" I asked.

"The English call me Angeni," she said, took the bowl and placed it on the ground. She reached her hand toward my chin and cradled it. Leaned in, she tilted my head up and down.

I don't know why I didn't see it before now, maybe because my heart was racing from my escape attempt, or 'cause the hut was so dark. Her eyes were a bluish color with strange white patches across them. I realized that Angeni was, for the most part, blind.

She put her fingers from one hand on my face and traced my chin, my lips, my cheeks, and my nose. She felt my forehead, the bandage, and ran a finger through my hair. "Hmm," she said. "You have beautiful hair."

"Everyone says I have my mama's nose and my dad's hair. I mean, his is brown, and mine is dirty blonde, but we both have hair that's super thick. Like, no one in my family will being needing Rogaine any time soon," I babbled.

Oh jeez, I sounded like a moron, but Angeni smiled. I didn't want to stare at her but the past couple of days had been strange. But I didn't think she could see me all that clearly. Fine, call me terrible.

Angeni had high cheekbones and deep-set eyes. She was tiny, lean, and fit. She could have been in her sixties, or even in her seventies. I couldn't tell. That's when she pulled the gauze bandage off my forehead and poked at my wound.

"Ow." I flinched.

"This is nothing: a flesh wound that's getting better, and a small knock to your brain. I can fix that. If you are to be a warrior one day, you must first learn to become a Messenger. And if you are to be a Messenger, you must gain knowledge of the differences between pains that steal lives, and those that are merely irritating."

Why did Angeni think I would want to be a warrior one day? The only warriors I'd be doing would be yoga poses. The only messengers I knew were those people who earned twenty bucks an hour plus tips, weaving their bicycles through the Loop's traffic to deliver documents, fruit baskets, or bad news. No way I'd ever be a messenger.

"I know for a fact you have been through far worse than this, Abigail," Angeni said. She dipped her fingers into the crock filled with her concoction, and smoothed it on my cut.

It stung and I cringed.

"This will help you heal," she said. "You will have a small scar, but every Messenger needs a marking. Otherwise, how would other Messengers recognize her?" She smiled.

My heart had calmed down, and my head did feel better. "I don't think I'm a messenger. I don't think I'm supposed to be here," I confided. "My name's not Abigail. I don't even know who she is."

"Fascinating. You and Abigail look so much alike, that you could be sisters," Angeni said. "Tell me more."

"I haven't met anyone from here until a couple of days ago," I said. "And no one will even tell me where I am."

She frowned. "You look like Abigail. But you do not talk or act like her. Share with me your real name and where you are from."

Angeni got it. Someone in my dream got it. I felt so relieved. "My name is Madeline Blackford and I'm from Chicago, Illinois," I said.

"How old are you?"

"I'm sixteen."

"Just like Abigail," she said. "Maybe you are long lost relatives. You lived miles away and never met."

"The problem is, Angeni, I'm from Chicago, probably hundreds of years after this time." *Whenever this time was*, I wondered. "We don't wear the kinds of clothes people wear here. We don't live in little huts, or houses with wooden forts around them," I said. "And we don't wake up to find everyone around us bloody and dead, unless we are in the military, or there's been a terrible, natural disaster or a terrorist attack."

I stood up and paced, agitated, around her hut, all twelve feet of it. "Which, thankfully, doesn't happen all that often, and has never happened to me before," I said. "Until now."

"This never happened to you before?"

"No. I've had my share of bad dreams, but nothing like

this. Everyone's treating me like I'm an idiot," I said. "They think I just hit my head, or that some Reverend needs to pray over me."

"Hmm. There is a metal rod on the ground close to you. Find it and stir the fire for me, please."

"Sure." I'd stirred fires before. Like, well, some time in my life. I found the rod, picked it up, and poked the fire.

"The fire is not your enemy. You do not need to attack it," Angeni said. "Just move the wood a little so the fire can find the driest parts of the branches, and burn them more easily."

"Okay," I grumbled and swooshed the rod around the branches and logs a little less violently.

"Do you want me to call you Abigail, or Madeline?" she asked.

"Call me Madeline!" I said, thrilled. "Would you tell me where I am?"

She sighed. "You are in a province in the Americas called Rhode Island. You were rescued from the Endicott settlement that was brutally attacked during a war. You do not remember any of this, Madeline?" she asked.

I shook my head. "I live in the United States of America. We have fifty states and one's called Rhode Island, but I've never been there." *Think*, I said to myself. Colonial outfits. A War. People who talk funny. "Am I in the Revolutionary War?"

Angeni shook her head. "No. You live in King Philip's War. People on both sides are very upset and have old angers, fears, and grudges."

The fire sparked under the kindling I had shifted and the flames started licking their way upward.

"There are so many hateful feelings that I do not believe this bloodbath ends any time soon."

How many wars had happened that I'd never heard of. Hundreds? Thousands? Good for me this was just a dream.

Bad for Angeni that she believed she was living during a brutal war. But—"Who is King Philip?"

"The son of the great Wampanoag sachem Massasoit."

"A Native American chief?" I asked.

"The great Indian chief who welcomed the colonists to these shores, and helped them so at least some survived the first winter," she replied.

"But now they're at war?" I racked my brain to say the right thing. "I'm so sorry. Everyone here must be very scared." I was thrilled this was simply a dream.

Angeni took my hand and squeezed it. "Whether they admit it or not, everyone in this war is terrified. But you are not dreaming, Madeline. You left behind your life in Chicago in future years when you traveled here. You are living, just like the rest of us, in the year 1675 during King Philip's War. A conflict I fear, many of us will not survive."

Did she just say what I thought she said?

"Are you telling me that I traveled over 300 plus years back in time—for real?"

She looked up. The dim light from the fire made the white patches covering her blue eyes look like morning mist.

"Yes," she said. "For real. Elizabeth is here. It's time for you to stop running, and help her."

There was a thumping and shaking of the skins covering the entrance to Angeni's hut. "Abigail!" Elizabeth hollered.

I jumped and looked at Angeni. "How'd you know?"

"Come visit me again." She covered the top of the medicine bowl in fabric and tied some twine around it. "Messengers need to learn the art of communication. Be nice to Elizabeth." She handed me the bowl. "No matter how many times she calls you Abigail, she still cares about you."

She kissed me on my cheek, turned, and opened the flap of her door.

Elizabeth stood there with Daniel and she didn't look very happy.

"I made some healing balm for Abigail's wound," Angeni said as we stepped outside her hut.

"Thank you, Angeni." Elizabeth grabbed my arm and marched me away from her hut.

By the time I swiveled and looked back, Angeni had already vanished inside her tiny home.

CHAPTER 11

*M*e, a time traveler? Me, with the anxiety who couldn't move through a crowded room without breaking out into a sweat, was supposed to be a Messenger? Me, who could barely cross bridges or climb a ladder? Did this sound like someone who catapulted through years, and careened through lifetimes?

Someone had a screw loose here, and that description usually applied to me. But this time I was going to sit back and see how this whole scenario played out, because this just couldn't be true.

Even though I was apparently living in the middle of a war, the next week was filled with the most awful to-do list of tedious, boring chores. Elizabeth let me sleep in until a little after dawn. Each morning I woke up to the sounds of a few roosters, hens, and animal noises instead of city buses and the TV news. My breakfast consisted of tasteless, blechy gruel.

Every single day I had to wrap my head around the crazy fact that I was still here, living in a freaky, colonial garrison during a war I'd never even heard of. Although I did get an earful about King Philip and his family.

His dad, Massasoit, was the Wampanoag Native chief who welcomed the colonists to America years earlier. He even celebrated the first Thanksgiving with them. He managed to keep the peace with the colonists for years, and apparently handed them a lot of land during that time.

When Massasoit died, his eldest son Alexander became chief. He was young, strong, and the colonists didn't trust him to keep the peace. They captured and questioned him. But by the time they released him he was terribly sick, and died on his way back home. Just about every Native on the east coast believed the colonists had poisoned and killed Alexander.

His brother, Philip, became chief. But after that, there really was no peace. Just compromise and suspicion.

Elizabeth and her crew made me do Abigail's regular chores: churning butter, spinning wool and making candles. When it quickly became obvious I had no talents in all these departments, (although the butter churning thing could be a great upper body sculpting work-out if properly updated,) I was demoted to simpler tasks—like carrying firewood, stirring stews, feeding the chickens, and sweeping floors.

On the days Elizabeth taught the children, I was supposed to help out by keeping an eye on them. Considering everyone in this garrison thought I was whacked from the attack, apparently I was supposed to keep my crazy eye on them.

Thanks to Angeni, I could now stir a fire and keep it going. Slamming! If I were really lucky, my upcoming SATs would include questions on all these subjects.

I'd been at the garrison for about ten days when my "sick girl" reprieve was over, and I had to be interviewed by the Reverend Wilkins.

Elizabeth made me put on a very proper dress (*translation: the ugliest dress ever*) and marched me down through the village across the commons to the church.

A couple of townspeople stared at us because I was still the subject of local gossip. I'd already guessed that Abigail wasn't the nicest person in the world. So they were pretty curious to see what had become of her. And what became of her was, unfortunately, me. Sorry Abigail. (*Note to Self: Karma's a bear.*)

Elizabeth and I stood in front of the church. It was a wooden structure, bigger than the garrison's houses and huts. It was located close to the commons, not too far from the stocks and other tools of punishment.

She leaned toward me and tucked a few wisps of my hair back under my white cap.

"Do I have to do this?" I whispered.

"Yes. The Reverend keeps asking everyone I know about you," she said. "'Has Abigail recovered? Is she still righteous? What if the demons claimed Abigail's soul during the Endicott attack?' The questions are exhausting."

"Tell him to stand in line, and take a number. Lots of people have asked about me before," I said. "What's the worst they can say?"

Elizabeth frowned. "They can say the only reason you are living is because you are a spy for King Philip or that you are a witch. They'll hang you for both."

"Oh." It seemed being labeled different wasn't trouble-free in any year. People would make your life a living hell in the year I came from. But in the year 1675, they would torture and kill you.

"So if I tell this Reverend guy what he wants to hear?" I asked. "Will this make life easier for us?"

"Yes, absolutely," Elizabeth replied. "I know things have not been simple for you since the attack. Reverend Wilkins is very smart. I do not ask you to lie to him." She looked me in the eyes. And then glanced quickly away.

She totally wanted me to lie to him. Assure the Reverend I was Abigail. After ten years of having panic attacks, and awful anxiety, the white lies came a little easier.

"Miss, you're on the floor of a Bloomingdale's dressing room. Do you want me to call an ambulance?" the store clerk asked when I was twelve and lying smack-dab on my stomach after a panic attack.

I looked up at her and didn't blink an eye. "Oh gosh, no. I'm just looking for my contact lens."

Now I peered at Elizabeth. She bit her lower lip, just like I did when I was nervous.

"Do you think you can do this, Abigail?"

I thought about Stanley Preston and what a tool he was. I would deal with the Reverend. "Piece of cake." I squeezed her hand.

We walked into the tiny church filled with a few hard, wooden pews, an aisle that ran up the middle, and a narrow, wooden pulpit about two steps up in the front.

Reverend Wilkins was waiting to interview me. He was that tall, skinny guy with the silver, greasy hair I nearly took out during my escape attempt in the garrison's commons.

"Come here, young lady," he commanded, and gestured briskly toward him.

"Yes, Reverend Wilkins." I looked at Elizabeth, who nodded.

I walked up the short aisle. We stood face to face. Not good because he had really bad breath. Did they even have dentists here?

He pushed my hair back and examined the pink scab on

my forehead. "Hmm," he said. "Your gash heals. What is your name?"

"Abigail Endicott."

"What year is it?"

"1675," I said.

He frowned. "Who is our sovereign King?"

"Our King is…" Oh dang, I didn't know that one. "King Simon Cowell the First." The former American Idol judge was English after all.

Reverend Wilkins glared at me squint-eyed. But I had answered two out of his three questions correctly. "King Charles II," he said.

"King Cowell, King Charles. I've been mussed up a bit lately. You are so smart, Reverend Wilkins. You knew what I meant to say." And for some reason—I curtseyed.

Elizabeth pinched my arm and covered a smile. Then she frowned and composed herself into a proper, uptight, colonial woman.

The Reverend harrumphed. "I am keeping an eye on you, Abigail."

"Yes, sir, your holiness, sir," I said.

His eyes narrowed. "We are not those unholy Catholics."

Elizabeth's eyes practically rolled back in her head. I'd screwed up again, as my parents raised me in the non-denominational church of God Loves You whoever your God is.

"What's a Catholic?" I widened my eyes innocently.

Reverend Wilkins looked constipated and mumbled something. "I trust you will be attending services this Sunday?"

Elizabeth and I answered in unison, "Yes."

"Thank you Reverend Wilkins," she said and took my arm. "Thank you very much for your time."

We exited the church ladylike and proper. We held our heads high and walked so slowly that all we needed was a casket to complete our funeral procession.

As soon as we were out of his sight, Elizabeth grabbed my hand. "Follow me." We tromped around the back of the church, passed some tiny houses, and entered an area lined with rickety, lean-to stables and small muck-filled pastures occupied by a few thin cows, chickens, and some goats.

She dropped my hand and peeked around—there were no people in sight. She lifted the bottom of her skirt up several inches off the ground. "If there are no persons present, I usually lift my dress up a little when we go through this part of the village," she said. "That way, I do not have to wash it soon thereafter."

"Got it." I hiked my skirt over my knees and followed her.

Elizabeth glanced back at me, looked horrified and stifled a giggle. "No! Not above your knees, above your ankles. You are not allowed to show your knees."

"You've got to be kidding me."

"No. Was all the sense knocked from your brain during that attack?"

"Maybe some sense got knocked *into* Abigail's brain," I said. "You colonial people need to lighten up."

"Right now *you are a colonial woman*," she said. "I don't know if the Abigail I knew will ever come back. But the Abigail that you are now needs a place to relax. Where you can think, breathe, and escape from all the eyes that stare upon you."

She led me to a dilapidated barn. A bigger barn door was closed and latched. She pushed open a short, tiny door next to it, and we ducked down to enter.

It was pretty dark inside, and it took a few moments for me to see clearly. The barn was a small, earthy, musty space filled with a few, thin bales of hay, some stalls, a horse, and a goat.

She stuck her hand in a bucket and then walked over to a stall halfway down the only aisle in this shack. She petted the head of a large, chestnut brown horse with a thick, black mane. "Hello, my friend," she said and let the horse eat from her hand. "Good appetite, Nathan. Are you feeling better today?" He flicked his tail while Elizabeth stroked his mane with her other hand.

For some reason Mama had insisted I take riding lessons when I was young. Those stopped after the accident. These gorgeous animals seemed too tall, big, skittish, and made me nervous. I didn't even volunteer at horse rescues. I stuck with the dogs and cats at the animal shelters.

But Nathan was stunning. I grabbed two handfuls of oats from the bucket. "Do you think he would let me feed him?"

Elizabeth smiled. "Is Reverend Wilkins an arse?" We giggled.

I held the flat of my hand out to Nathan who tickled my palm with his lips as he nibbled. When his huge tooth grazed my hand, I yanked it away. The horse looked at me and I swear, he rolled his eyes and quietly harrumphed.

"Go on now," Elizabeth said. "Nathan is a good horse. He will not bite you. Give him what's left in your hand. Everyone deserves a second chance."

I held my palm out to the horse again, closed my eyes, and stiffened my shoulders as his lips grazed my skin.

"I know you are still healing and have these outbursts," Elizabeth said. "I realize this has been a difficult time. But I have been tough with you for a reason."

"Explain, please?" I asked.

"When your mother decided to re-marry, and move back to England with your brother, you refused to go. You were thirteen-years-old but you declared you would not step one foot on that ship," she said.

This was definitely Abigail's life memory, not mine. But I needed to know it. "Tell me the story, Elizabeth." Nathan bumped my empty hand for more food and Elizabeth suddenly looked sad. "Please tell me the story, *again*," I said.

She lumbered back to the feed bucket. Seemed like her pregnant belly grew bigger every day. "You said you felt like you had important things to do here in the Americas. Things to learn, possibly even share with people some day."

She grabbed several handfuls of oats and returned to Nathan. "I told your mother I would look after you, school you, Abigail. I even promised her I would marry you off some day," she said as Nathan nibbled the oats. "Everything was good until you left to live with the Endicotts over a year ago."

"Oh," I said. "Why did I leave?"

"You do not remember?"

I shrugged my shoulders.

She sighed. "You met someone, you would not tell me who. This person encouraged you to be independent and take chances. This person said that you had the power to change things in the future."

"That sounds a little crazy," I said.

"I know. But you were always very strong-headed."

"Me?"

Elizabeth smiled. "You used to love it here, in this barn. You told me you could think your thoughts and plan your plans without any of us worriers interrupting you. The animals calmed you. It was so quiet, you could even write in the pages of your book."

Whoa. Abigail had a book that she wrote in? Even the

school kids Elizabeth taught, who I basically babysat, didn't have actual books. "Where's Abigail's book now?" I asked and watched Elizabeth's face fall from happy to sad. "I mean, where's *my* book?"

"I do not know. You always hid it." She sighed, walked toward the door and opened it a sliver. "Stay here a while longer. Maybe this place will help you remember who you are, as well as where you left your book. But, you must return before nightfall." Elizabeth ducked her head, squeezed under the opening of the short doorway, and left.

For the first time since I landed in the year 1675, I was alone.

CHAPTER 12

I stroked Nathan's mane and gingerly handed him an old apple I had pocketed earlier from a basket of withering fruit in Elizabeth's food storage area. Abigail had a book. Was it like Mama's book? Could it have clues to help me get back to my real life? My head was spinning, my brain raced.

I needed to unwind. I needed to think. The only thing that did that for me back in Chicago was yoga. I looked around the stable. Yes, it was a little stinky, and the space was cramped, but why couldn't I do yoga here?

I realized I could. I could do things for myself in this foreign world. I would still be Madeline Blackford, who just happened to be transported back in time three hundred plus years—hopefully just for a short while.

I spotted some blankets piled in the corner of the barn, grabbed one, and tossed it on the earth in front of Nathan's stall. I put my hands flat on it and stretched my body with my butt up in the air, my face inches from the blanket.

My nose twitched and I sneezed. Phew, this thing smelled

horsey. *(Note to self: pretty much everything smells horsey in the year 1675.)*

Technically, this yoga pose was Downward Facing Dog. Right now it was Downward Facing Colonial Girl. I stretched my spine, grunted, and felt a couple of lifetimes of stress roll off my shoulders.

"This feels amazing," I said to Nathan. "I wish you could try this."

He flicked his tail and blew through his lips loudly.

"Hah! Horse Breath! You're good." I blew through my lips, too. Horse breath was a great way to reduce stress.

I segued into more yoga moves: planks, pushups, back bends, and sun salutations. Those were my favorites. You'd lift your arms as far as you could over your head and thank God, the stars, the heavens, or whomever you cared about that you were doing this practice.

I tried to sweep out negative emotions, and pull in positive energy as I lengthened my spine and expanded my ribs. I breathed deeply. Inhaled. Exhaled. I knew each breath could help wash away my anxiety.

I broke into a sweat, my endorphins kicked in, and I felt great except for the fact that the ugliest dress in the world was squeezing me half to death. I looked around. No one was here; only a few animals. Elizabeth had said we could do things a little differently, if no people were watching. I made the decision.

I finagled my way out off my long, ugly dress, and tossed it across the barn.

I was in my pilgrim underwear. These were definitely not Victoria's Secrets—more like Victoria's Rejects. They were hideous, fluffy pajamas with a big girdle around the middle. The girdle, called a corset, was most likely damaging my organs, and I was done with it.

I reached behind my waist and yanked on the cords that kept this thing cinched around me. Loosened them enough that I pulled myself out of this torture device, swung it around my head and pitched it through the air. "See ya, wouldn't want to be ya." The corset landed in a corner of the barn with a *thunk*.

I felt my ribs expand. Freedom. I closed my eyes, and took my first Warrior pose since I was back in Chicago. "Warrior One," I said. My front knee was bent at a ninety-degree angle with my back leg extended, and my arms straight overhead. I breathed, held the pose then shifted my pelvis and stretched my arms out long in both directions over both my shoulders.

I felt fierce and fiery. I breathed deep and guttural. For the first time in weeks I felt in control. "Warrior Two, Nathan. What do you think?"

Someone started clapping. "Those are the scariest, warrior moves I have seen in years," a young man said.

I shrieked, and whip turned. Samuel leaned against the far wall of the barn, his arms crossed in front of him, a grin on his face. He wore colonial pants, and a white shirt that was unbuttoned below his collarbones. His black hair was pushed behind his ears but a few thick curls fell above his shoulders.

"How long have you been here? Are you following me?" I glanced around the stables to find my clothes that I had thrown, apparently, everywhere. Great. "That is just wrong!"

"I was here before Elizabeth and you entered. I did not want to interrupt you. But since you are officially a warrior, what are you worried about?"

"I'm not worried." I jumped up, snatched the world's ugliest dress off a bale of hay, and tried to pull it over my head. But got caught in it.

My right hand was stuck in the left sleeve. I was pulling

this stupid dress on backwards. I struggled to yank it off me, twisted it around, and dressed while my cheeks popped bright red.

Samuel tapped me on the shoulder. "Let me help you with this."

"Back off!"

He did. His hand flew off my shoulder like he'd accidentally touched a lit burner.

I heard a loud *rip* as my arm popped out of the waistline of the dress that wasn't sewn securely. "Don't look!" I hollered and tried to pull my arm back in.

"Yes, Abigail." He covered his eyes, and sat back on the barn's floor shaking in laughter. "Because you are so charming, I will do whatever you ask."

"Are you always a jerk? What are you doing in here?" I twisted the dress and pushed both my arms through the actual sleeves.

"Actually I came to check on Nathan."

"Because you're such a nice guy." I smoothed my dress, glanced down and saw a hole in the waist about the size of a fist. Oh no, I looked like a complete idiot. I covered the hole with my hand, smoothed my hair back and looked at Samuel. But he wasn't sitting in the aisle anymore.

Samuel was in Nathan's stall. He whispered in his ear and applied ointment from a jar, just like the one Angeni gave me, to a wound on his flank. Nathan whisked his tail and stomped his front foot. "Shhh," Samuel said. "You are getting better."

"What happened to him?" I walked toward them but definitely stayed outside of his stall. That was one tall horse.

"War wound," Samuel said. "He was General Jebediah Ballard's horse."

"Elizabeth's husband?"

Samuel nodded.

"How did he get hurt?"

"Jebediah rode with fifteen of his men to meet with the Plymouth colonists to strategize battle plans. They were ambushed by Philip's warriors, not far from here, in a corn field."

"Oh." My hand that covered the hole in my dress flew to my chest. "That's why Elizabeth is so afraid."

Samuel nodded. "Nathan was struck by an arrow that pierced deep into his shoulder. Even though he was in great pain, he carried his master back home. He saved Jebediah." He stroked the horse's mane.

"Nathan was determined," I said. "He has a strong, loyal spirit."

"Some people believed it was a miracle. Others thought it was lucky, but a waste," Samuel said. "There was great debate whether Nathan should be put down."

"That's ridiculous. I've spent enough years in animal rescue to realize you don't discard a soul, just because it is not perfect."

"A lame horse with an infected leg is a burden during a war. They do not have time or efforts for charitable causes here."

I realized why Elizabeth wanted me to do well with the Reverend.

"But you're trying to save him," I said.

"Not just save him. I want him to be strong again. I want him to be able to go back into the unknown, maybe frightened, but still follow his horse nature." Samuel looked at me. "Which is to be a messenger."

Whoa. Angeni said I was a Messenger. "What do you mean, 'a messenger'?"

He scratched Nathan's nose, massaged his neck, and worked his hands down to the horse's shoulder. "The Great

82

Spirit taught us horses are strong, animal messengers. If a person has horse as his totem, he has the power and endurance to deliver powerful messages."

Nathan flinched, and stepped away from him. But Samuel didn't chase or crowd him. He just stood and waited. "This will make you feel better," he said and whispered words to Nathan in a language I'd never heard before. "Trust me."

The horse eyed Samuel, took a few steps toward him and lowered his head. "Good boy." Samuel put his face next to his and rubbed more salve around the wound.

I reached my hand over the paddock gate and petted Nathan's head. "You're a hero, Nathan. You must get better quickly."

Samuel placed his hand on top of mine. "You are different since the attack."

"Is that a good thing or a bad thing?" I asked and realized his gaze was direct. He looked me straight in the eyes.

"It is a good thing."

My heart pounded. Oh jeez, could a teenager have a heart attack? "Okay." In the near distance, a bell clanged loudly and I jumped. "What's that?"

"Means there is news." Samuel slowly released my hand. "We gather at the commons. Remember?"

"Right," I felt my skin tingle where his fingers had touched me. Was this my over-sensitivity thing, or something I'd never felt before, and didn't even have words to describe? I walked toward the barn door.

"Abigail?"

My heart pounded and my face burnt, and I had the strangest magical feelings. What if he said he liked me since the day we met? I meant *me* as Abigail. I turned toward him. "Yes, Samuel?"

"There is something you need to know."

Those hazel eyes of his were doing a number on my brain

and I think I actually squinted when I looked at him. It was kind of like looking at a really bright star in the sky, on the blackest of nights. "Yes?"

"You forgot this," Samuel said, and tossed the corset to me.

CHAPTER 13

The courier who delivered the news that day on the commons was a twenty-something guy, with a bad case of acne, wearing filthy, colonial clothes. His job was to share war updates with the various colonial communities fighting Philip's war.

The garrison's people huddled together in small, clubby groups to hear his report. I could practically touch the anxiety hanging in the air.

The courier's news wasn't great. The garrison's men had traveled south and met up with more colonial soldiers to battle Philip's warriors. But no one seemed to know or could figure out where Philip or his men were hiding.

That's because they attacked quickly: raiding and burning settlements. There were a few full-blown battles. But not one that Jebediah or the garrison's men had engaged in. It seemed like a case of hurry up and wait. A collective sigh of relief rose from the crowd, that none of their men were missing or dead.

But the courier had more to report. "Your relatives might be safe—for now. But one must be careful. Philip's spies are everywhere. They recently kidnapped Patience Donaldson, a pious woman, as well as a pastor's wife. They hold her hostage, even as I give you this message."

There was a flurry of excited mutterings. Elizabeth shushed the crowd and asked, "How do you know Mistress Donaldson is alive?"

The crowd quieted, and the courier regarded Elizabeth, dubiously. "We know. I cannot tell you how or why," he said.

"Do you negotiate for her release?"

"I cannot answer any more questions, Mistress Ballard," he said and walked away accompanied by the Reverend Wilkins. Several young men in the village, including Tobias, Samuel's friend, followed them, and seemed to hang on their conversation.

I looked at Elizabeth. Her face had turned ghost white, almost gray, and she clutched her stomach.

I put my hand on her shoulder. "All things considered, the news was pretty good, Lizzie. You okay? Can I help?"

"I do not think so." She shook it off, and stood up straight.

Sunday came, and as we promised, Elizabeth and I went to church services. The church was packed with the women, children, and the few men left in the garrison as well as the handful of Natives that the colonists deemed "friendly".

I had learned that the colonists called the friendly Natives, "Praying Indians." Just like every second-class citizen in any culture, they were not only expected to attend services, but could only do so if they stood at the back of the building.

A grayish rock veined with white quartz crystal that was bigger than my fist rested on the Reverend Wilkins's pulpit.

It functioned as a paperweight, and held down his sermons and other scribbling.

Reverend Wilkins shook his Bible a lot, (another possible upper body workout,) and lectured about the wages of sin, religious freedom, and the dangers of leaving the old country for the new land.

The old land held the threat of religious persecution, imprisonment, and never ever being able to strike out on your own. Unless you were nobility, you couldn't own your own land and had to pay ridiculous taxes. You were basically a peasant, which meant you were poor and screwed for your entire, relatively short, miserable life.

The new land called The Americas, held the promise of gold, riches from the fur or silk trades, and you could actually own land. You'd have to work that land, have religious freedom, but had to commit to a tough life filled with harsh weather, hard labor, and awful farming conditions.

During the first hour, Reverend Wilkins lectured about piety, piousness, and hating one's enemies. He segued into we are right, and they are wrong, and perhaps there was a hidden advertisement in there somewhere for hemorrhoid crème.

That's when I felt Elizabeth bump my arm with hers 'cause apparently I'd dozed off. My head rested on her shoulder as I woke with a start, and heard muffled snorts from the back of the church. I swiveled my head and saw both Tobias and Samuel elbowing each other while they tried not to laugh.

I glared at them, and made the universal sign for 'Zip it,' across my lips.

Elizabeth frowned, and nudged me again.

The Reverend Wilkins paused in the middle of his sermon, and squinted at me.

I widened my eyes to beyond innocent standards, and

pretended to touch my lips as if a wisp of hair had landed on them.

The Reverend harrumphed, and then preached for another butt-numbing hour.

———

Elizabeth and I left the church with the rest of the garrison's inhabitants. Many of them seemed to be rubbing their behinds or stretching their backsides. "Tell me it's not always this bad. Tell me we don't have to do this every Sunday," I said.

"We have to do this every Sunday," Elizabeth said.

"I can't take it."

"You always have in the past." Elizabeth nodded and smiled at all the people, primarily colonists, as well as a few Praying Indians, who stared at us, curious. "I need you to say something nice to just one of these people," she whispered into my ear. "I would like to be rid of the witch rumors."

"What!" I said. "That's just crazy talk."

"You have been very different, Abigail, since the attack," she said.

Well of course I've been different. *I wasn't flippin' Abigail and I'd never lived in the year 1675.*

"If convicted of being a witch, they will drown you or hang you."

I shuddered. Neither sounded appealing. "Fine. How do I put the kibosh on the witch rumors?"

"Compliment some of the women. For example, Mistress Powter." Elizabeth delicately nodded in her direction. "She is the woman with the unfortunate wart on her chin. But she is the best weaver in the garrison. She made the blankets that covered you when you were sick."

I scanned the crowd and spotted the wart-chinned lady.

"Mistress Powter!" I said. "Awesome to see you here. Wasn't that an exciting sermon?" Out of the corner of my eye I saw Elizabeth bite her lip.

Mistress Powter eyed me suspiciously. "Yes, Abigail?" The five chatty, middle-aged women hovering around her eyeballed me too.

Suddenly I felt like something that was about to be squished onto a slide and examined under a microscope in biology class at Preston Academy.

"I am so remiss in thanking you, Mistress Powter," I said. "My sincerest apologies. I have been recovering. Your warm, wool blankets helped me heal when I was sick. You are extremely talented, Mistress Powter. With wool and weaving and… blanket making. Thank you."

She paused and then nodded at me. "You are welcome, Miss Abigail." She beamed and walked away, while her friends surrounded her and clucked.

"Not a witch," one of them said.

"Not smart enough to be a spy," another replied.

"Still addled," a third woman chimed in as they walked off.

Elizabeth patted my arm. "That was perfect."

In the near distance, Tobias grinned at me, and slugged Samuel on the arm.

Samuel caught my eye and winked.

Oh my God. My skin got tingly and I felt a little light-headed for a few seconds. (*Note to self: pull it together. Don't be a dork.*) I gave my brain a mental shake. Maybe if I could fit in for a while without getting killed, I'd find the way back to my real life. I thought about Samuel and my heart did flip-flops. Maybe, before I traveled back to my real life—maybe I'd even fall in love.

he days rolled by. I helped Elizabeth with the chores and reined in the school kids. Every other day I'd find an excuse to go find some quiet time at the barn. Where I'd secretively meet Samuel.

We talked about how Nathan was getting better, what my life was like with Elizabeth. He told me he lived with Angeni —that she was like a mother to him. I asked him what happened to his parents, but he just shrugged and shut up. Didn't seem like he wanted to talk about it.

One day he asked me to teach him the yoga warriors. So I did.

"Watch me," I said and took a Warrior One pose. And yes, I was fully dressed this time.

"I am watching." He massaged Nathan the horse's neck, shoulder, and leg. "Have you seen a stronger warrior, Nathan?"

I willed myself not to blush. "Do you really want to learn this?" I asked.

"Yes."

"Then come over here and do what I'm doing."

He did, but his alignment was awful. His knees weren't lined up, and his hips were definitely off.

"No." I tapped Samuel's knee with my finger. "Bend your front knee so it lines up directly over your ankle," I said. "Otherwise, if you practice poor form for any length of time, you will totally screw up your knee. Then you might need arthroscopic surgery or something."

"No surgery." He shook his head. "I heard that is torture."

"Arthroscopic surgery's not that bad."

"The father of my friend was shot during a battle. The doctor performed surgery. Cut off his leg to save him," he said.

I winced. "That's awful. How long was he in the hospital?"

"The doctor took his leg on the battlefield. He still screams at night when he hears the sawing sounds in his head."

I think my blood pressure plummeted, and I probably turned deadly white, as Samuel grabbed my hand and squeezed it. "Show me more Warriors."

"I don't know." I felt a little queasy. "Maybe I should go." Go back to the clattering of el trains, TV, movies, the Internet, my school, friends, and family. Back to modern times where they did surgeries in hospitals.

He placed my hand on top of his knee. "Stay. Show me."

I felt the muscles in his leg. He was so strong. He placed a finger under my chin and tilted it up, so I looked into his eyes. He was beautiful. His cheekbones were high, his eyelashes jet black and long, his nose regal, and his lips full. *I was doomed.*

Back at home, a guy as hot as Samuel would *never* be interested in me. He might say, "Hey," to me at a club if he knew I was a friend to Chaka, whose parents were music mogul gods. But he'd quickly move on and start checking out the models that were at all these events for schmoozing reasons. Then I'd never see or talk to that guy again.

Samuel put his hand on my cheek. "Where are you?" he asked.

"I was just thinking about my home," I said.

"What about your home?"

"I really miss it. Is that crazy?" I asked.

"No. The Endicotts were good people," he replied.

"Not the Endicotts." I flashed to those first moments I woke up on that blood-soaked ground surrounded by all the colonists who had been slaughtered. Which was also the first moment I laid eyes on Samuel, as he surveyed the scene, me, and then disappeared into the woods with Tobias.

"You are not Abigail, are you?" Samuel asked.

Dang. There was no way I'd be answering his question.

"Warrior Two." I pulled away from him. "Stretch your back leg behind you, and turn your heel slightly in."

He did.

I reached down and adjusted his heel. "Now extend this arm." I tapped his left arm. Amazing sensations flooded my body. I felt like I'd downed a shot of honesty mixed with a chaser of courage.

It was coming through Samuel to me. Why wasn't I meeting his magical soul back in Chicago? I was increasingly overwhelmed by desires to be with him for real. *(Note to self: not the best idea to fall for a guy who lives three hundred plus years before you were born.)*

"What do you want me to do now?" he asked.

I was still holding onto his arm. Oops. My hand flew off him. "Sorry!" What did I want him to do? *Be real for me,* I thought. *Do not vanish; don't disappear.*

"Abigail was never nice to me. She kept to herself, had secrets she did not share," Samuel said.

I covered a cough. "Maybe she changed. I mean I changed.

Stretch your arm toward, um, the door and your other arm in the opposite direction," I said. "Toward me."

He did. "Do us both a favor. Tell me your real name?" He asked while he mastered a perfect Warrior Two pose. Strong, fierce, sexy. The only thing left for him to perfect the pose was—

"Right," I said. "Turn your head, and face out over your front arm."

"Show me." He closed his eyes and waited.

Samuel was in an almost perfect lunge. How was it possible that this mysterious guy and I could have this chemistry, this connection? Perhaps I was the only one feeling it. Maybe he was just meant to be a friend or a mentor, or worst-case scenario, temporary, like Brett.

"Breathe, Samuel." I placed my hands on each side of his beautiful face, and turned it toward me. Nathan whinnied and stomped his foot. "Open your eyes. You're new to yoga. You don't want to fall."

His blinked his eyes open. Our faces were inches apart. "Sometimes falling can be a good thing."

"Oh."

"I promise you." He took my hands in his, and placed them on his chest on top of his heart. "I promise you, I will tell no one. I will keep your secret. Tell me your real name and where you are from."

A few seconds passed but they might as well have been hours as my heartbeat drummed in my ears. "My name is Madeline Blackford," I said. "Madeline Abigail Blackford from Chicago. Illinois. Over three hundred years in the future." I ripped my hands from his, and ran out the door.

***

Even though all I could think about was Samuel, I didn't go

back to the barn for a couple of days. My feelings bounced all over the map. I was petrified of making a jerk out of myself.

It's not like Samuel could google me. But what if he changed his mind and thought I was crazy? I didn't think I could take that right now.

So I buried myself in household chores and helped Elizabeth. Lucky for me that her school had several new students.

Elizabeth was smart, clever, and educated. She was a gifted and compassionate teacher to twelve colonial children. They sat on small, rustic, wooden benches gathered around the fireplace and clutched their little, handmade books. I learned they were called hornbooks—a wooden paddle with some papers stuck on top.

I was supposed to keep an eye on the kids as I cleaned up the fireplace, swept the floors, gathered and stacked wood, helped stir pots, and flipped meat on the grill.

"What country did we come from?" Elizabeth asked the kids.

A couple of hands went up. "England!" a new little schoolgirl blurted.

"Very good. Thank you, Miss Smythe," Elizabeth said.

My head whipped around so fast I thought it might spin off my shoulders. I stared at this brown-haired girl with a large nose. She looked awfully familiar.

"Who is our King?" Elizabeth asked.

"King Charles II!" the brunette munchkin said. My mouth dropped open as I recognized the kid was a younger, innocent version of Taylor Smythe. But without the nose job. How bizarre.

"You are the best teacher ever, Mistress Elizabeth!"

Elizabeth smiled. "Thank you, Miss Smythe."

The Smythe doppelganger raised her hand and waved it furiously. "Mistress Elizabeth! Mistress Elizabeth!"

"Yes, Mary."

"I do not believe Miss Abigail is stacking those logs next to the fireplace properly. They could fall over and start a fire," Mary Smythe said.

I stared at the Smythe munchkin. And remembered what a pain she was. Definitely some past life karma playing out. I caught a questioning glance from Elizabeth.

"I'll happily re-stack the logs should you want."

Elizabeth nodded.

I looked at the logs, sighed, and took them down off the pile—one by one. Just when I thought things couldn't get more absurd or complicated—they did.

"Work on your letters, children. And we will see you next week," Elizabeth said.

Another week had passed without my dad, or Sophie, or even Jane. Did they miss me? Were they looking for me? Would Dad give up on me eventually, like he finally gave up on Mama? Oh God, I hoped not.

I suffered through another grueling Reverend Wilkins' sermon. It amazed me that these same colonial people who traveled across an ocean to do back-breaking work, expose themselves to weird diseases, hideous weather, and fight brutal wars, could still find the patience to listen to some pompous guy drivel on for hours. Don't get me wrong—I pray to God all the time. But my God teaches love and forgiveness.

Elizabeth and I left the church. "Reverend Wilkins is such an—"

"No. No. Do not say it." Elizabeth patted her stomach, which seemed to be growing about an inch each couple of days. "Look at the stocks," she whispered.

I did. There was a guy shackled to its bottom with a large

95

iron clamp around his leg attached to a chain. He looked miserable. "I have been here a day," he said. "Will not someone feed me?" Most of the churchgoers walked past him, and said nothing. A few laughed. I carried an old corn cake I had planned to give to Nathan. I handed it to this guy instead.

"Thank you, Miss," he ripped into it.

"What did he do?" I whispered to Elizabeth.

"He did not attend church services for two whole weeks in a row."

"You've got to be kidding me."

Elizabeth shook her head.

Mistress Powter walked past and smiled at me. I nodded back and ground my teeth in a forced smile. "I'm going to explode," I whispered.

"Go to the barn for a bit," Elizabeth said. "You are always calmer and happier when you come home from the barn."

CHAPTER 15

She was right. I grabbed some oats, opened the gate to Nathan's stall, and squeezed inside. This was the closest I'd ever been to a horse since before my accident. He looked tall. Frankly, he looked massive. He nudged my hand with his nose. "Yeah, got it. Someone's hungry."

I fed Nathan the oats, and then massaged his neck tentatively. "You're so normal," I said. He pushed his head into my hand again, his eyes at half-mast. He was darling. "How come everyone here isn't more like you?"

I laid my head on his shoulder, wrapped my arms around his neck and hugged him. Funny, the horsey smell didn't bother me anymore.

"I do not see you for a bit, Madeline, and you have already fallen for a far nobler soul than I," Samuel said as he entered silently through the door.

My breath caught in my throat. Nathan regarded Samuel and nodded his head. It was an awfully big head. He whinnied and stomped his front foot on the ground. I felt a little jittery and backed away until I was pressed flat against the side of the stall.

"He likes you." Samuel climbed the gate and dropped into the stall. "You do not need to be scared of him." He murmured something to Nathan and examined his shoulder. "And you, my friend, do not need to be scared of her."

"I'm not scared." I squeezed out of the stall door.

"I would be if I were you." He lifted Nathan's front hoof on the injured side and took it through range-of-motion exercises. "Strange place, different time. I think you are doing very well for someone who has traveled so far: over three hundred years and many miles."

"What do you know about time traveling?" I asked. "You know about traveling and you've been holding out on me?"

He sighed. "I suspected. But I did not know for sure until you confided in me, Miss Madeline Blackford from the future." Samuel smiled the most gorgeous smile I'd ever seen on a guy.

"Well then, you must share. Immediately," I said. "This traveling thing is completely new to me. I don't know what I'm supposed to feel or do. How to act, what to say." And it hit me. "Oh, my God. Are you a traveler, too?"

"I am not a traveler. Angeni is convinced my future lies elsewhere. I know people who travel, but cannot tell you who they are without betraying promises and secrets," he said. "So I think we should leave this stinky barn, and you can tell me about your life in the future."

"But won't the garrison's people freak if they see us together?" I asked, and immediately felt like an idiot for pointing out the obvious. "I'm sorry. But they seem uptight about, well, everything."

"Mmm. Good point." Samuel climbed up to the top of the stall's gate, reached his hand overhead, and pushed a board in the barn's ceiling. "So we create a distraction of sorts." He banged on the board. It dislodged after the third hit. A cloud of dust, as well as some remnants of bird nests rained down upon us.

I ducked, and covered my head with my hands. "Is this your distraction?"

Samuel caught the worst of the debris and coughed. "More like my plan of attack. Now that I know the warriors."

Feathers and twigs stuck to his hair and shirt. I couldn't help myself and I giggled. "Nice look. Are you okay?"

"I don't know what the word, 'Okay' means. But I will say yes. I am healthy, but feel a little feathery." He handed me a skinny, old-fashioned book.

I sucked in my breath. "Abigail's book?"

"Yes," he said as he pulled debris from his hair and brushed it off his clothes. "To answer your question, you, 'Abigail', will work on your book, while I exercise Nathan in the pasture outside the barn."

"Come here," I said.

He raised an eyebrow but stepped toward me.

"You have a twig sticking out of your hair." I pulled it out.

"If anyone believes it odd that we are keeping company, we have a very good excuse."

"Which is?" I was not going to let go of that twig. I was keeping it.

"You are writing about how General Ballard's courageous horse, Nathan, was injured during King Philip's war, and now heals."

"You rock!" I raised my fist to bump his. But he looked at me, confused. "Just bump my hand, okay?"

He did. And smiled again.

I sat outside on a bale of hay next to a simple log fence that surrounded a small pasture. Abigail's book was open on my lap.

At first Samuel let Nathan check out the pasture without a lead, all on his own. Nathan walked tentatively, sniffing the yellowing patches of grass that remained.

I was torn between watching them, and examining the book. What did she write? Were there clues in here?

After some time, Samuel approached the horse. "Come on, brave one. You need to move those legs." He led Nathan back and forth across the pasture, examining his gait. Seeing where his muscles seemed to catch.

"In the future," Samuel asked, "does everyone dress very fancy? Do the men and women wear wigs, like the English? Which I believe to be hideous."

My mind shot to Chaka and Aaron, and the makeover they gave me, where they turned me into an overly made-up, trollop wannabe. "Actually people dress pretty strange in the future. Fashion changes every season, and most people can't keep up with it."

"How are my pants and shirt?" Samuel asked and plucked at them.

Smoking hot as long as it's you who's wearing them, I thought. "Fine," I said. "You look styling. You'd almost pass for a guy living in my time."

"What about the town you live in? It is probably larger than the garrison, with bigger houses." He smiled and let Nathan rest.

"Almost three million people live in Chicago. Many homes are smaller, like mine. But some people, like my friend Chaka, live in skyscrapers—buildings so tall they almost touch the sky. Like the John Hancock building—it's one hundred stories."

Samuel shook his head. "How do they fashion wood strong enough to build that?"

"They don't use wood. They build with metal, and glass, and other materials."

He shook his head and patted Nathan on the shoulder. "What about transportation? I dream about the day that everyone, no matter their lot in life or their heritage, is able to ride in comfort."

"Well, that's a whole 'nother thing," I said and paged through Abigail's book. "Plane travel's much more difficult since 9/11. TSA, long lines, and waits at the airports. But you can still fly thousands of miles in just a few hours. Amtrak trains still run. People in the cities generally use public transportation like buses, subways and L trains. Suburban commuters will carpool or hop on their local railways like Metra. Most peeps grab a cab or take public transportation if they're in a city. Because gas prices are up, the big trend now is a car that is energy-efficient. Like a hybrid that gets great gas mileage."

Samuel stopped in his tracks and regarded me completely confused. "I was thinking that everybody would be able to ride a horse in the future."

Oh no. I'd gone off on a tangent. "Yes. Everyone can ride a horse in the future, Samuel. But that's not our general way of transportation."

"Do you think I'm simple-minded?"

"No," I said. "I think you are kind. I think you are amazing." *I think you are stealing my heart.*

"Do you have family there?" He resumed leading Nathan around the field but seemed preoccupied.

"Yes. My dad, stepmom, and my little sister."

"A stepmom?" he asked.

"After my mama had been gone a long time, my dad married another woman. Sophie's like another mom to me. I adore her."

"What kind of work does your father do?" he asked.

"He helps heal people."

"Like Angeni."

"A little different," I said. "But he's still really smart and talented."

"What's your sister like? Pretty like you?"

I tried not to blush. "Jane's younger than me. Cute. She's a pain, but I miss her."

Samuel jogged next to Nathan who picked up his pace. "I bet you miss everyone. Do you miss the young man who courts you? The one you are promised to?" he asked. For once, he wouldn't look me in my eyes.

"Not really," I said. "There is no promise between us." And Brett definitely no longer 'courted' me.

"Oh," Samuel said.

"Can I ask you a question?"

"Yes."

"What were you and Tobias doing in the woods at the Endicott settlement?"

He turned and regarded me. "What do you think we were doing?"

"I don't know."

"Do you think we hurt those people?"

The first few times I saw him, I asked myself those same questions. But now? "No."

"Elizabeth sent us ahead of her search party to be scouts, and to defend against any warriors who might have stayed behind." And then he was quiet and worked silently with Nathan.

"Are you angry with me?" I asked.

"There is nothing to be angry about."

"But you're not talking to me now."

"I have talked with you more than I have talked to anyone, besides Angeni."

I scanned Abigail's book looking for clues, and waited for

him to pick up the conversation. It didn't happen. Dusk came and went. It was past time for me to get back to Elizabeth. "Well, you let me know, when we can, you know, talk again," I said.

He nodded his head abruptly and led Nathan to the barn.

"Thanks for the book." I followed him.

"You best be going."

I trekked back to Elizabeth's house. The weather was getting cooler, and I pulled my cloak around my shoulders tightly.

Homecoming weekend had probably come and gone at Preston Academy. I wondered if Chaka was elected Homecoming Queen. Did Aaron miss me? We probably would have been each other's dates this year, 'cause Brett was most likely going with Brianna, and I didn't think Aaron had met anyone new.

But I'd been gone a while, and maybe he had. I hoped he met a sweet, cute guy who adored him. Life had changed, and moved on without me. And I realized—I didn't care about Brett anymore. There was no sadness, no worry, or pit in my stomach. Brett could have gone to Homecoming, Prom, or even the moon with the beautiful red-haired girl, or an Irish potato for all I cared. I felt like a huge weight lifted off my shoulders.

I walked in the front door of Elizabeth's house. "I'm here." Shrugged off my cloak with more energy than I'd felt in weeks.

"I have been waiting for you," she said.

I always got home before dark. One time I was late.

"Abigail?"

"Just a minute." I tried to hang up my coat on the peg on the wall.

"I do not believe I have a minute," she said. Elizabeth was collapsed on the floor next to the fireplace, clutching her stomach and grimacing. The school kids were gone, she was alone and her face was white as chalk.

I skidded onto the floor next to her. Her skirt was scrunched up toward her waist, and there was the smallest bit of blood on her hand. "Are you okay?" I asked.

She grimaced and contracted forward in pain. "A colonial girl should never be out at nighttime," she said. "Go fetch Angeni. Now."

CHAPTER 16

*T*raced through the garrison toward Angeni's hut. This was completely different than the first time I bounced around this place during my botched escape attempt. It was nighttime, and the fiery torches stuck in the earth tilted all over the place, and barely lit the surroundings. The shadows in this camp jumped out like monsters in a horror movie, and I tried not to cry out.

After sundown, most of the residents were already inside their homes. Hanging out after dark wasn't encouraged. I sped past the church and spotted one guy on sentry duty snoozing, as he slumped against the tall, wooden fence that encircled the garrison. Great. We were so protected.

I passed more houses and huts. Angeni's hut lay in the corner, right next to the fence. I stopped myself from plowing through the thick skins that made her front door, and lifted my hand to knock. I heard chanting and singing in a foreign language coming from inside.

I pulled back the skins a half inch, peeked and caught an eyeful: Angeni was twirling in circles, just like mama used to do in her small office lined with books. Her arms and face were lifted toward the heavens as she chanted words I had never heard before; her long, silver, unbraided hair flew through the air along with her skirt that spun around her ankles.

"Sa. Ta. Na. Ma," she chanted. "Sa. Ta. Na. Ma." She looked magical. For a second I forgot she was blind because I swear her eyes that gazed toward the heavens were a clear, brilliant blue.

I hated to interrupt her, but Elizabeth was bleeding and emergencies always beat out good manners. I slapped the thick skins that made up her door with my hand. "It's me, Madeline," I hissed.

Angeni pushed open the flaps and gazed toward me with clouded eyes. "What is wrong?"

"Elizabeth is bleeding. She needs you."

"Grab my big bag on the right, a bit away from the fire. Hurry."

I did and we left in seconds.

I tried guiding Angeni back to Elizabeth's house through the darkness. But honestly, she led me. We arrived at the house in about half the time it took me to reach her.

Angeni kneeled next to her on the floor, her hands palpating Elizabeth's stomach. "Do you feel the child?"

"I do not know. I had the pains, and I saw the blood." Elizabeth hyperventilated, while sweat dripped off her forehead.

Angeni leaned in and whispered into Elizabeth's ear. She then said to me, "We need to be alone right now. Wait outside, Madeline. Take your cloak. There is a chill in the air."

"Are you sure? Maybe I can help?"

"Help by doing what I ask," she said. "I will send you a message when it is time for you to return."

Fifteen minutes went by. I had no watch but a half hour must have passed. I was freaking about what was wrong with Elizabeth. My throat grew tighter by the minute. I couldn't afford to have a panic attack here. There was no Xanax in 1675.

I rubbed my hands together, and decided this had to be a case of bad nerves. I just needed to burn some energy. My mind flashed on the swimming pool at Preston Academy, and I remembered what it felt like to slice through the waters, doing lap after lap. But the garrison didn't have a swimming pool.

I tromped back and forth in front of her house. That helped a little. I lifted my skirt above my ankles, and jogged in circles around Elizabeth's house. That burnt some anxiety. I wish I could go to the barn and do yoga, but it was too late and too dark. And you weren't supposed to be out after dark if you were a colonial girl during King Philip's war.

I wondered if anyone here would know what to do with a person having a full-blown panic attack, except maybe for Angeni. She was inside the house helping Elizabeth with life and death issues. During my thirteenth trip around the house I almost plowed into someone.

Tobias stood directly in front of me as I rounded the corner. I stopped in my tracks before I tackled him.

"You look panicked," he said. "What is wrong?"

I put my hands on my knees, tried to get my breath back, and looked up at Samuel's best friend.

Tobias was handsome in a rough-around-the-edges way, and seemed like a nice enough guy. We'd never spent time together but he always smiled at me. I had never gotten an emotional read on him—for good or bad. Frankly that was fine by me, 'cause there was enough going on. But I wasn't going to share anything about Elizabeth. That felt private.

"Don't know, Tobias." I bounced up and down on my heels. "Have you lived in this garrison for a long time?"

He nodded. "My father was schooled by Reverend Wilkins and is counsel to General Jebediah. We've lived many places. Met many people. But we always return here. This garrison is home to me during this wartime. It is a good place to call home."

Tobias could travel to other places. He was comfortable here, but I wasn't. His father was important and he belonged to the community of people that lived in the garrison. I was just another misfit. I shook my head, stood up, and turned away from him 'cause if I teared up—I didn't want him to see.

"What's wrong?"

"I don't think I belong here."

"Maybe you belong here, maybe you do not. I think that you forgot who you are. Give this place more of a chance," he said.

I heard the faint howls of wild animals in the distance, and shivered.

"Just wolves. They won't hurt you. They want nothing to do with you," he said.

"How do you know?" I asked.

"My father is a powerful hunter. He trained me since I was a child." He stepped closer to me. "Hunters learn patience, details. They pay attention to the sounds around them. Notice footprints in the earth. The wolves are predators. But they won't bother you, unless you behave like prey, or they are very hungry."

I looked up at Tobias, and my breath caught in my throat

again. More of my stupid anxiety. Strange how I had never even registered this guy before now. He was incredibly dark and dangerous, and I wondered about the jagged scar on his cheek. But I didn't want to ask him about that. He might get offended.

So I tried to think of something that wouldn't piss him off. "You and Samuel seem like best friends," I said and blew on my hands.

Tobias smiled. "In some ways we are more like brothers. You need to warm up."

My eyes widened. "No really, I'm fine."

"Let us walk."

"I don't think I'm supposed to leave here," I said. "Besides, a walk's not going to make me feel better."

"Yes it will. Angeni will let you know when you can go back inside. In the meantime we can walk around the inside of the fence." Tobias leaned in and whispered, "Because a colonial girl cannot run without everyone believing she is crazy."

I looked at him and decided. Yes, I wanted to feel better. Yes, I would walk with Samuel's best friend.

"One lap and that's it," I said.

CHAPTER 17

*A*fter four laps, Tobias and I alternated between fast walking and jogging around the inside of the garrison's tall, wooden-spiked walls. Lucky for me, most of the garrison's residents weren't out at night, as I knew they wouldn't appreciate seeing a colonial chick huff and puff around their fort's perimeters as she jogged next to a Native teen, even one dressed in colonial men's clothes.

I didn't hold up my skirts; I just plowed forward and breathed. Tobias didn't keep up with me. He was actually a yard or so ahead of me, and jogged backwards. This guy was freaky athletic.

"Why do the wooden fences that surround this village lean inward?" I asked.

"It is more difficult for attackers to crawl up them during an assault," Tobias said.

"Why do the Praying Indians have villages close to these walls?"

"Because even though they have been converted, the colonists still distrust them," Tobias said. "Should there be an attack on this garrison, the Praying Indians will be killed first."

Oh great, I thought, and my stomach turned. "Why do you get to live inside the garrison with the colonists?" I asked, and hated those words as soon as they fell out of my mouth.

My dad and Sophie raised Jane and me to be adamant about equal rights for women, minorities, religions, as well as people who were rich and poor, and all of us who fell in-between. I felt like I'd just asked a completely bigoted question. I felt like a jerk.

"Because we are lucky enough to have ties to important people in the garrison," Tobias said. "We have skills they do not have. So they want to keep us close. Let us sit for a moment." He pointed to the hanging platform elevated about four feet off the ground that loomed in the town's commons.

I shook my head. "No way, I'm sitting where people get killed."

"No one has ever been hanged there," he replied.

"Fine." I said. We trudged over and sat down. "Why are you being nice to me?"

"Because I want to get to know you better. Besides, Samuel is intrigued with you. The new Abigail, I mean."

"Oh." I felt my cheeks flush. Hopefully Tobias wouldn't see that at night.

"He likes you," Tobias said. "He told me."

His words made my heart pound, and I got the shivers. I heard the wolves howl and I gazed up at the moon. The clouds looked like they were competing with each other to race across it.

"You like him, don't you, Abigail?" Tobias asked. "Or whatever your real name is." He smiled at me.

No way I was going to tell him my real name. "I don't

know what I like," I said, and in the distance heard Angeni call my name. I sprang to my feet. "I've got to go."

"And I will escort you."

We left the town commons striding briskly past the church and the stocks.

"I thought you were not going to return until Angeni sent you a message," he said.

"She did."

"Oh." He blinked, but kept a straight face.

I realized I hadn't heard Angeni's message out loud. *I heard it in my head.*

At Elizabeth's house, I feared the worst, but hoped for the best. Before I could knock on the door, Samuel opened it.

I stood there for a heartbeat, and stared up into his strong face, which frankly, right now, appeared irritated. "Is Elizabeth—"

"Where were you?" Samuel asked.

"I was just—"

"I was protecting her, " Tobias said.

"She does not need your protection." Samuel frowned.

"Boys, be quiet. Come inside, Abigail." Angeni motioned to me from across the room.

I couldn't see Elizabeth, but I squeezed past Samuel. I practically felt the chill come off him. Tobias was right behind me.

"We do not need the cold night air in this house," Angeni said. "Samuel, go home. Tobias, I do not want you two leaving the garrison tonight."

"Yes." Tobias nodded at her.

"I mean this," Angeni said. "No matter what your reasons."

Tobias left with Samuel following him. They shared a

glance that didn't appear all that friendly. But I guess friends who were more like brothers weren't always on the best of terms.

"Elizabeth?" I asked.

Angeni leaned over the fireplace. "She sleeps in the back room."

"They're okay?"

"For now. Elizabeth needs rest and quiet, if she is to keep her child. You must be starving." She turned from the fire, placed a plate on the floor, and pushed it toward me. "Eat."

I swallowed hard. "Can I see her first?"

Angeni paused, then nodded, and pointed to the back of the house. I headed that way when suddenly she was next to me and whispered in my ear, "Walk quietly, Madeline."

I tiptoed into the tiny back room where they kept barrels of food supplies and sundries. Angeni had made it comfortable with cushions and warm throws. Elizabeth slept on the same mat I laid on weeks earlier, covered in the same blankets.

Her face looked peaceful. She didn't seem to be in pain. I listened to her breath. It was regular, not raspy. I turned to leave, but something grazed my leg. It was her hand.

"You were brave tonight," Elizabeth said. "Thank you."

I took her palm and squeezed it. "You're the brave one, Lizzie."

I felt Angeni staring at me. Her face was a map that I was learning to read. She didn't frown. She didn't smile. Her face just appeared enormously practical. I understood that it was time for me to leave Elizabeth alone.

"Dream sweet dreams for you and your baby," I said. "Tomorrow's another day for the both of you." I put my fingers to my lips, leaned forward and placed that kiss gently onto her forehead. "I love you." But she was already asleep.

Angeni and I sat on the floor across from each other in front of the fireplace and ate from metal plates. "I saw you..." I wasn't sure how to explain what I saw. "At your home. I saw you twirling in circles. You chanted words I've never heard before. 'Sa-Ta-Na-Ma.' Are those Native words?"

Angeni shook her head. "Not Wampanoag words." She checked out my plate, which was empty. "Eat some more." She took my dish and ladled more meat and stew onto it.

"That's enough." I waved my hand. "I can't get fat."

"Fat?" Angeni smiled. "You are learning, growing and if you are to be a Messenger—I need you to be stronger." She added a pinch of herbs to the top of the stew, stirred it and handed it to me. "Fat. Hah!"

"Okay." I worked on my second helping. It was delicious. Maybe it was the herbs. I wondered again what she meant about the Messenger comment, but realized I need to know something else first. "Tell me about Sa-Ta- Na-Ma?"

Angeni sighed and leaned back against the wall next to the fireplace. "Come here." She patted the floor in front of her.

I scooted over and sat in front of her, my legs crossed. She reached forward and held my hands with hers. "Touch your thumb and tops of your second fingers together, and say the word, Sa."

I did. "Sa," I said. "What does it mean?"

"Sa means forever. Infinity. Some souls meet. They fall into hate, or crash into love and chase after each other, through different bodies and lifetimes. They are meant to be together, but must first learn lessons in order to figure out how to do that," Angeni said. "Touch your thumbs to the tips of your third fingers and say, Ta."

Wow, that was very cool info. I did as she asked. "Ta."

"Ta stands for 'life,'" Angeni said. "The life we have now, as well the lives we create through our thoughts and prayers, and actions. Past lives, future lives. Touch your thumbs to your fourth fingers, and say—"

"Na." I touched my thumbs to my fourth fingers.

"Na means death. A physical death, or the end of a strong pattern, a way of life. Touch your thumbs to your fifth finger tips and chant—"

"Ma." I touched the ends of my pinkie fingers to my thumbs. "What does Ma mean?"

"Re-birth," Angeni said.

"Does this mean that our souls are reincarnated?" I asked. "Does this mean that our souls are forever?"

"Each soul's destiny is not the same. Nothing is pre-determined. Not one soul's legacy is written in blood, etched into stone. Some souls will change, and could become immortal. Others who do not learn the lessons, will not," she said. "Time and lives collide and jump. Sometimes, we have not been properly schooled, or trained to know the best decisions to make. To take the strongest actions."

A sinking feeling flooded my brain and it felt like Novocaine descended through my body. "I'm caught here in some kind of past-life, aren't I?" I asked. "Technically, I'm not Abigail, but I'm also not completely Madeline, either?"

"You need to grow strong." Angeni pointed to some blankets in the corner of the room. "I know it is not as comfortable as your other bed, but it will have to do for tonight. Sleep now. Build strength."

Not before I got an answer to my question. "If I am Abigail as well as Madeline, it seems like I am both these people, but not either."

"That is right," she answered.

"But then, *who am I?*"

She squeezed my hands and said, "You are a Messenger."

CHAPTER 18

I *smelled burnt sage, lavender, and freshly baked chocolate chip cookies.*

Our car was smashed off the edge of the parking garage with enough force that the front tires catapulted up and over the guard wire. My cookie flew through the air, just like Mama's head that smacked the windshield and whiplashed backward.

From the back seat I could see the front of our car dangling: we balanced high in the air between the garage and the riverbank below it. I screamed.

Mama looked back at me, her head bleeding as she struggled with the seatbelt. "Hang on, Madeline!"

"Mama!"

Blood dripped down her forehead while she twisted like a pretzel and finally unbuckled her seatbelt. She crawled over the front seat into the back and leaned over me as the car wobbled.

Her hair brushed against my face as she worked like crazy to get me out of that booster seat. "Shh baby girl. It will be okay."

I reached my hand up and pushed back her hair that touched her brow covered in sweat and blood.

"No matter what happens, I will never lose you." Mama fumbled to unlock all the gizmos that strapped me in. She unsnapped two, but I couldn't stop sobbing. "You're my good girl, Maddie." Mama wrangled the last buckle. "We're almost out of here."

That's when we were rammed hard from behind again, and jolted forward.

I woke up, startled, and gazed into Samuel's face as he squeezed my shoulder. "You cried out in your sleep."

"Oh. A nightmare," I said. Actually more like I just remembered a huge chunk of the accident. What was going on? Why now after all these years was I finally remembering?

"We need to leave now," he said. "It's past dawn, and we cannot be gone for long."

I looked around. "Where's Angeni?"

"With Elizabeth. She needs us to gather plants for her medicines."

"Where?" I asked. "Back in her home?"

"No," Samuel said.

I was outside the garrison's walls for the first time since Elizabeth rescued me from the massacre. They probably lugged me through here, but I remembered nothing because I was drugged up and had a concussion. (*Note to self: don't expect to remember much of anything following a major accident.*)

Samuel led me down a narrow, trampled, earthen path that wound through fields where the grasses came up to my waist. They were yellowing, and dying from the cold weather. I reached out and touched some. They felt brittle in my hand, and snapped in my grip.

"How far are we going?" I asked.

"Only far enough to get what is needed for Angeni's medicines," he said.

The air was crisp, the sky overhead a perfect blue. I caught a glimpse of dark forests in the distance. I heard the faint roar of some kind of water and smelled a salty, ocean breeze. I felt peaceful out here: liberated from the confines of the garrison, free from anxiety and worries. Then my gaze fixed on Samuel's back as he walked several yards in front of me.

"Hey Samuel," I said. "You're talking to me again."

"It seems like I have to, or I will never experience a moment's peace," he said. "We have a small climb ahead of us."

"Hey!"

He turned toward me.

His face was flushed, his hair loosened and curled around the collar of his opened white shirt. This moment segued from feeling great to feeling perfect. "I like being here," I said. "With you."

He turned away, but not before I saw him smile. "I like it, too."

We walked silently through a lush, dark, pine forest, while the sounds of cascading water drummed close by. Mist sifted through the canopy of pine needles above us. The occasional ray of sunlight danced on the forest's floor illuminating acorns, fallen branches, and leaves that looked like jewels.

"What happened to your parents?" I asked.

"The woman who gave birth to me was shipped back to England soon after I was born," Samuel said. "Her family did not approve that she had relations with a Native man."

"So, did your dad raise you?"

"For a while." He frowned. "But he was killed in a hunting accident when I was young."

"I'm sorry. My mama disappeared when I was young, too." On the outside Samuel and I couldn't be more different. But in some ways, we were very much alike. Why couldn't I have met him in my real life? Why did I have to meet him in this weird time travel thing?

I tripped, and my legs flew out from beneath me. I saw the ground rise up under my eyes. "Oh." I reached my hand forward to break my fall.

But Samuel grabbed my shoulder and spun me around. He caught me and pulled me close to him. My heart beat quicker, and I was dizzy for a moment as my face pressed into his shoulder.

"Thank you."

"I need to teach you how to walk on this land." He released me. "Each step you make is an imprint. Choose where you step, as well as how hard your body weight comes down."

I practiced choosing my steps until we approached, and stood too close to a cliff that overlooked a wide expanse of air. The view across it was another treacherous overhang with a choppy, white-watered river that lay hundreds of feet below.

I flashed to Mama's head smacking the windshield as we dangled between earth and sky. "You go ahead. I'll stay here," I said. No way was I moving an inch further onto that cliff.

"Angeni said that if you made it this far, you could make it all the way. Scrape the bark from the tree next to the river, while I find the plants she wants."

"I'm happy to scrape the bark from any of those trees over there." I pointed in the opposite direction of the cliff.

"But…" He frowned.

"I am not stepping one foot closer to that drop-off," I said. "Heights are scary. People can fall and get seriously hurt."

"You just fell and I caught you."

"Not from a fall like that." I pointed to the cliff's precipice. "People lose their lives if they fall from that kind of height." I backpedaled. "Don't you get it? We're not all strong and invincible. We are flesh and blood. People can disappear for good, forever. People you love will never be seen again. You will never share a meal, laugh about something silly, touch someone's face, or even have a chance to tell them goodbye," I said. "I'm not getting anywhere near that cliff."

"Whatever you say, Madeline. Whatever you want." He walked off.

I felt like I had ruined my perfect day. "Samuel, wait!" I took a few steps toward him.

Samuel whipped around, his eyes scanned the forest, and he pulled a knife from a sheath on his belt. "Get down. Now."

CHAPTER 19

I dropped to the ground, and crouched.

Samuel peered at the forest behind me. "Show yourself."

Tobias popped out from behind a tree, about twenty yards away. "I did not want to move too suddenly," he said. "I know, brother, that you do not like to be startled."

Samuel put the knife back. He held his hand out to me and helped me stand. "Why are you here?"

I dusted the dirt off my skirt, and a wave of anxiety washed over me. I felt nervous, antsy. I'm not sure I cared why Tobias was here, because suddenly I didn't want to be here.

"Angeni sent me. She wants the mushrooms," Tobias said. "She doesn't want you and Abigail coming back a second time. Too dangerous."

Samuel frowned. "After I am done gathering the—"

"Where are the mushrooms?" I asked, as my throat tightened. My anxiety was kicking in. Not good.

"Close to the caves," Tobias replied.

Samuel shook his head.

"How far away are the caves?" I asked.

"Minutes," Tobias said.

"No," Samuel said. "Abigail is not going to the caves."

"Any heights involved?" I watched Samuel's face turn to stone.

"Not like these cliffs," Tobias said.

"Let's go."

"No! You wait here with me," Samuel insisted. "Tobias can collect them on his own."

Samuel was dreamy, strong, and complicated. But right now he was one more person telling me what I could, or could not do. I glared at him. "Thank you for your concern. But I'm not going to sit around here and wait for a panic attack." I walked toward Tobias.

"I promise that I will not let her out of my sight," Tobias said.

"Be quick about it."

I could practically feel Samuel's eyes pierce the back of my head like psychic daggers. Apparently, I hadn't made him very happy today.

———

Tobias and I walked a safe distance away from the cliffs and the river deep below it. "Thank you for accompanying me," he said.

"I have to keep moving, or I'll have a meltdown."

"Meltdown?"

"Pressure, worries, old fears, you know?" I said and he nodded. But did he get it? Probably not. "How far away are the caves?"

He pointed to a large mound of rocks a short distance in front of us. "Did Samuel tell you about what happened to him in that river below?"

"No."

"He only shares that story with people he trusts," Tobias said. "Still many tribal people and colonists know it. I'm surprised you do not."

Samuel didn't trust me. Was I being too difficult? Again? "What happened to him?"

Tobias shrugged. "I will tell you, only if you promise to give me something in return."

Like what? I didn't have any money. Didn't seem to have any luck. I'd happily hand him my corset, but I doubted he'd be into that. "I have nothing to give you."

"Of course you do," he said. "You have secrets."

"I don't know what you're talking about." *I totally knew what he was talking about.*

Tobias frowned. "Many colonists believe that Native babies have demons in them, so they created a test to determine which children were innocent. They stole the Native babies from their parents, and threw them in a river. The 'pure' babies would float. Those with the devil in their hearts would sink and drown."

I shook my head. "That's definitely urban legend."

Tobias shook his head, confused. "When Samuel was six-months-old, his mother was forced to sail back to England without him. The colonists did not know if Samuel was a white baby or a Native baby," Tobias said. "So they threw him in the waters of that river that rushes at the bottom of the cliffs below us. Then they watched to see whether he would sink or float."

"You're lying!" I said. "The colonists would never be that cruel."

"You are indeed delusional if you think only one tribe of people is capable of cruelty."

"I still don't believe you." We approached the caves.

"It does not matter what you believe. What matters is the truth. Now help me find the plants Angeni asked for."

I was sick to my stomach. Colonists drowning Native babies were too grisly to imagine. Did they still do this? Did Elizabeth know that they did this? My hands shook as I helped Tobias dig the mushrooms up from the earth.

He collected them in a rough cloth sack.

"You're Native. Were you thrown in the river?"

"No," Tobias said.

"Why not?"

"Because my father is very powerful, and has strong alliances with the colonist leaders."

Samuel interrupted us and helped us finish all the digging, scraping, and collecting. We were all silent. The mood had turned sour.

The trip back to the garrison was completely different than the journey out. Samuel didn't talk to me. He and Tobias shared a few words in their Wampanoag language. Frankly, they were both too serious, and I wanted to bolt far away from them to process everything I just heard.

As soon as we were back inside the garrison's gates, I thanked Samuel and Tobias coolly, and walked away from them as quickly as possible. I needed to talk with the only sensible person in this whole place: Angeni.

We sat next to each other in her hut while I helped her prepare the herbs to dry. "The colonists would never do something that awful." I wrapped some plants with thick twine and hung them to dry on rough hooks snagged onto the ceiling. "They are not barbarians."

"For once Tobias spoke the truth," she said.

"It's just not possible."

"I witnessed it, Madeline. A small group of colonists gathered on the shore. The Reverend Wilkins himself tossed Samuel into the waters."

My hand flew to my chest. "That's awful!" My eyes welled. The thought of Samuel not being here because of the colonists' cruel and hateful superstitions—it made my head spin, and my heart sink. "I don't believe for one second only "pure" babies floated. That's insane. How did Samuel manage to live?"

"A Messenger sent word to Samuel's father about what the colonial radicals were planning. He traveled great distances to be there at that place and at that time. He appeared out of nowhere, jumped into the river, fought the currents, and rescued him. In the eyes of the colonists—Samuel floated for enough time that he was considered pure," Angeni said.

She knelt next to a bench covered in furs, reached underneath it, and pulled out some clothing. I saw buckskin pants and shirts. I saw a fierce necklace made of shells, bones, and white feathers.

"His father took him until he was killed. Then the Wampanoag tribal elders and chief asked me if I would raise him," Angeni said.

"Why you?"

"I was childless, but wanted to be a mother. And I knew since Samuel was very young, that he had a gift for healing. I could help teach him."

"But that must have completely changed your life?"

She nodded. "It did. We didn't completely fit in with either the Wampanoag people, or the colonists. We lived away from people, on the outskirts of Native villages and colonial settlements. When King Philip's war broke out, Elizabeth and a few other friends insisted Samuel and I seek refuge, here, at the garrison."

"I'm so sorry," I said. "For everything the both of you have been through."

"Sometimes life requires you to make uncomfortable decisions. Do things you never expected. I have had much joy raising Samuel. Although he would never let me do something like this," she said. "Come here."

I went to her.

"Try this on." She draped that gorgeous necklace over my head.

"Is it for me?" I was dying to run and find a mirror, or anything shiny enough to see its reflection.

Angeni patted it, and a look of contentment shone on her face.

"No, Madeline. This is mine. It is part of my bloodline, my totem. I believe in time you will get your own symbol fitting for a Messenger."

"What is a Messenger?" I asked, looked around the room for anything reflective, as I had to see this necklace.

Angeni handed me a metallic cup. I squinted at the necklace that adorned my neck. It was so fierce, and it made me feel brave and powerful.

"Some souls are so close to the Great Spirit, that they can travel between time and worlds," Angeni said. "Most of these people do not even realize they do this. They think they simply have colorful dreams, imaginary friends, or hear voices when no one is talking directly to them. Others accuse these folk of being impractical. Say they are too sensitive, nervous, or flighty in nature."

"That sounds like me," I said.

"*It is you,* Madeline. That is why I am training you."

Angeni kissed me on the cheek, gently took the necklace from me, and returned it under the bench.

Everyone told me I was too sensitive, too much of a dreamer. Now, all those things I hated helped to make me a time traveler. "Why does the world need Messengers?" I asked.

"Because there will always be superstitions, anger, dread, and fear of the other," she said. "And some messages not only change lives but can save some. Time to check on Elizabeth. I did not tell her I sent you outside for the herbs. She only knows you were helping me."

"Oh. So, I shouldn't tell her I left the garrison?"

"You decide. She loves you, but she can be a little over-protective."

"Tell me about it."

"Someday you will feel the same way," Angeni said. "And since you would not get close to the cliffs today, I want you to practice the Sa-Ta-Na-Ma chant. And do something that makes you feel a little scared. Messengers grow their courage like herbs in a garden. The seeds are planted. The soil watered, the leaves pinched as the plants grow. A Messenger's skill and courage are not handed to them. They work for it."

"Okay," I said a little embarrassed that I'd been slacking.

I was half ways back to Elizabeth's house when I realized: I saw Angeni before either Samuel or Tobias did. How in the world did she know I didn't get near those cliffs?

CHAPTER 20

*O*ver the next week, Elizabeth seemed to be doing better. The cramping stopped, her appetite picked up, and she slept like a stone. I wished I could say the same for myself.

I went to the barn to practice the Sa-Ta-Na-Ma chant in private. I was surprised to see Nathan wasn't there. I hoped he was okay. He had seemed to be getting better, too.

I sat on the floor in a meditation position in front of Nathan's stall, touched my fingers and chanted, "Sa. Ta. Na. Ma." I thought about the words they translated to: Infinity. Life. Death. Rebirth.

Were Samuel and I chasing each other's souls through different lifetimes? What about the death and rebirth part? Had we been together in other lives? If so, how come I didn't remember him, especially now that he wasn't showing up at the barn today, and I already missed him?

I kept hoping he would suddenly appear. Laugh at me. We could do some warriors, talk, and just hang out. But he never showed up that afternoon. Or the next day.

A couple of days later, I took Abigail's book and went

down toward the pasture where Samuel had exercised Nathan. They weren't there.

I sat for a while, and paged through her book. Her handwriting was odd and there were little notes and scribbles. Nothing jumped out at me—maybe because I wasn't really paying attention. I just wondered where Samuel was. Dusk arrived a little earlier, as autumn stretched its way toward winter. Since Elizabeth's medical scare, I always left before it got dark.

I asked Elizabeth if I needed to visit Angeni for more herbs or medicines. (*Note to Self: invent better excuses to check on the guy you're crushing on.*) But she said everything was good. Her baby was growing. She felt big, bulky, but healthy. She just longed for Jebediah to come home.

I practiced the Sa-Ta-Na-Ma chant at the barn, but I didn't attempt anything new, or scary. It was bad enough that Samuel never joined me at all that week. Maybe he was mad at me, or tired of my anxiety, and all my ridiculous fears. I couldn't really blame him. I think the chant was supposed to empty my mind, and raise my consciousness. But, how could I do that if every other thought on my brain was about Samuel?

I woke in the middle of the night from the clatter of rain pelting the roof. It seemed the heavens had opened, and rain fell sporadically the next day while Elizabeth taught school.

When the bell in the town commons clanged almost as loudly as the siren on a fire truck, Elizabeth, the school kids, and I jumped. There was news.

Elizabeth's face turned white, and she bit her lip, but she held it together for the kids. "Children! School ends early today. We go to the commons and find your parents," she said.

"Grab you coats and your hornbooks. Don't forget to practice your letters," I said.

"Easy for you to say," Mary Smythe said. "You do not even talk like a proper, colonial lady."

"Whatever, kiddo." I wrapped a scarf around Mary's scrawny neck and whispered, "Don't think because I'm putting up with you now, that I'll be doing that in high school. Got it?"

She frowned. "Got it."

Elizabeth and I marched the kids down to the commons, and matched them all with their parents and guardians. The Reverend Wilkins was already preaching hell and damnation from the hanging platform above the ground as the crowd gathered tightly around him, anxiously waiting for the real news.

The skinny courier finally interrupted the Reverend. This time his news wasn't as good. There had been a battle in Hatfield, Massachusetts. It was bad, and it was brutal. Many folks, both Native and colonists, had been killed, and for the most part, Hatfield had been destroyed. The residents who survived, escaped to Springfield where the local colonists sheltered them.

General Jebediah and the garrison's men caught some action. A few men were wounded. Worse—one killed. The Reverend and the courier had visited that soldier's home, and informed his family before this public announcement.

The crowd hushed as everyone glanced around to try and figure out who wasn't there. Who had lost a husband, a father, a son? Who wouldn't be coming home ever again?

The women wrung their hands, their faces relaxing when they met glances of friends and neighbors. *That* son was spared. *That* husband would be coming home.

The courier plowed ahead with the rest of his news. He looked exhausted, and I think he just wanted to get his job done. Patience Donaldson, the pastor's wife who had been kidnapped was still in King Philip's custody. Her release had not yet been negotiated, although rumor had it, she was still alive. Again, we were cautioned that King Philip was a monster. We must be on the lookout for his spies and avoid danger at all costs.

The crowd dispersed, muttering amongst themselves. I saw Tobias walk off with the courier and Reverend Wilkins. He seemed to hang on their words. Angeni stood alone; Samuel had not accompanied her to the commons.

"I'm going to walk Angeni home," I told Elizabeth, knowing full well she could do that by herself. "If that's okay by you?"

"That is a good, kind deed that you do," Elizabeth replied.

"Thanks. I'm nice like that." Especially when I had ulterior motives.

"You do not have to do this, Madeline," Angeni said as I held her arm and guided her around some puddles, and muddy sinkholes, on the way back to her home.

"Yes I do." I definitely had to question her about Samuel's whereabouts. In a kind and gentle fashion.

"Have you practiced the chant since last I saw you?" she asked.

"Yes."

"Have you done anything a little scary or dangerous?"

"No," I replied.

"Why not?"

"Because…." What could I say here? Because I don't voluntarily visit the scary and dangerous places. Because I'm terrified to feel that way. *Maybe I don't want to feel at all.* "I'm scared."

"I am no stranger to fear," Angeni said. "It can paralyze a person. We can work on that." She squeezed my hand.

"Really?" I asked.

"Really," she promised. "Messengers still have fear. They learn to travel in spite of it."

We reached her hut and I knew Samuel wasn't there. His energy wasn't here.

"You seem sad. Do you want to tell me?" she asked.

"Yes. No. Yes. Is Samuel still here at the garrison?"

"Of course. He is with that injured horse," she said. "I think he might have healed that animal. Brought him back from the brink of death. Samuel has a healer's touch."

Angeni thinks I can be a Messenger. Angeni believes Samuel is a Healer. This was the best news that I had heard in what seemed like forever.

"Where is he?"

"Peek outside the gates," she said. "Go. Now."

I practically bolted for the garrison's gates. I caught a couple of irritated glares from the colonists, but I didn't care. As luck would have it, the two guards had the huge, wooden doors open a several feet, their eyes riveted as they watched some commotion happening outside.

That commotion was Nathan galloping in circles around the fort's steep walls, while Samuel rode him bareback.

"Samuel!" I yelled as they flew past the gates. He looked at me, his face flushed from the exertion of riding and guiding Nathan. He broke into a huge smile.

He slowed Nathan down to a canter. They turned, and trotted back toward me. "Abigail!" Samuel said. "Nathan is almost completely healed. Do you see how strong he is?"

"I saw! He's strong, and beautiful, and I am so happy!" I practically skipped outside, but a guard pushed his way in front and blocked me.

"No one's allowed to leave the garrison right now, Miss," he said.

Now was not the time to be holding me back. "But I just want to—"

"No one, Miss," the guard insisted.

I pointed to Samuel who had dismounted from the horse, and walked toward me. "But *he's* outside."

"He is exercising the General's horse," the guard explained, like I was an idiot. Right, most of the colonists still believed me to be an idiot ever since the Endicott attack. "Besides, he is a Native. You know the rules for Natives are different than the rules for colonists. You best move back inside and head home." The guard started to close the large gates directly in front of Samuel and me.

Separating me from him.

His mistake. I poked the guard hard on his shoulder. "That guy's my friend," I pointed to Samuel. "He just spent hundreds of hours nursing General Jebediah Ballard's horse back to health. And you want me to stay here and not talk to him—why?"

"I already answered that question, Miss."

Samuel was just steps away, and I knew he was listening in on this conversation.

We stood yards from each other. Nathan grazed on some yellowing grass and waited patiently. Samuel stared straight into my eyes. He was beautiful, strong, and I felt honored to know him in any lifetime.

"No worries, Miss Abigail," Samuel said.

"I'm happy for Nathan and proud of you, Samuel. You're gifted, truly a healer."

"As you are a Messenger." He walked back to Nathan.

I needed to be with him. I needed to see his face up close, talk with him, and feel his energy. When? How?

The guards were closing the gates. A guard said to Samuel, "You give us some kind of signal or holler when you're done with the horse, boy."

"Yes, sir." Samuel turned to me. "Miss Abigail?"

My breath caught in my throat.

"Yes?"

"Expect a message. Soon."

I had a hard time sleeping that night. Images of Samuel and Nathan raced through my brain. Samuel riding on Nathan's back, his leg muscles defined, his face proud, his hair flying, as he guided the horse he brought back from death's door. The horse he healed.

I also saw images of Nathan. His black mane bounced off his chestnut coat that rippled from the exertion as he galloped around the garrison's walls, seemingly happy to be strong again.

Sometime during the black of night, the wolves howled. No matter how many times I heard them, they always sounded eerie and gave me the shivers. They were most likely hunting. But not Nathan, thank God, as Samuel would be looking out for him, keeping him safe. I knew from my work with animal rescue that horses were nature's most magnificent and desired prey.

I finally gave up on sleep and sat on the floor, my back against the wall and chanted silently, "Sa. Ta. Na. Ma. Sa. Ta. Na Ma." I shut my eyes, touching my thumbs to my fingers, and thought about souls who chased each other for infinity.

What compelled them? What drove them? Love. Hate. Recognizing your soul mate. Could those souls ever find peace? Really be together? Exhausted, I rested my head against the wall.

A noise woke me. It sounded like a pebble bounced off the outside of the wall next to my head. I opened my eyes. Another pebble smacked the house. Five in all. I pressed my ear against the wall.

"I have a message for you," Samuel whispered, muffled from the outside. I shoved back a giggle, as I didn't want to wake Elizabeth.

"Be quiet," I said and heard Elizabeth snore lightly from her sleeping quarters.

"Hurry. I need to show you something."

CHAPTER 21

I snuck out of the house. It was nearly, pitch black outside. Just hints of the moon above us, but not yet the promise of sunrise. Samuel crouched in the bushes outside the house. "What are you doing?" I whispered.

He stood. "I have a surprise for you." He grabbed my hand. "Do you trust me?"

I had never trusted anyone more. "Yes."

"Then come with me," he said, dropped my hand and off we ran.

The guard that night at the garrison's gates was Daniel. He did not stop us or lecture me. He unlatched the gates, and allowed Samuel to silently lead both Nathan and myself out through a narrow opening.

"Thank you, Daniel," Samuel whispered, as we stood outside the garrison's safety.

"You healed Nathan. Maybe you can heal her, too." Daniel

nodded at us before he shut the very tall gates and latched them with several indiscrete *thunks*.

Wow. What a difference in attitude. No preaching, lecturing; just kindness. "What do you want to show me?" I asked Samuel.

He pointed to a large tree trunk nearby. "Watch this." He hopped onto the trunk, and then jumped onto Nathan's back.

"He looks so much stronger," I said in hushed tones.

"As do you," Samuel held out his hand to me from high above the ground.

"No, no." I shook my head, 'cause I realized what he wanted me to do. "I haven't been on a horse in years. Let alone at night without a saddle and wearing a granny skirt."

"We do not have the luxury of time."

"I can't jump that high. And if I did, I'd probably kick Nathan, and hurt him, and ruin all the great work you've done."

"Messengers need to be trained. Messengers need to travel despite their fears." He pointed to the sawed-off trunk. "It is close to the ground. Climb it, grab my hand, and I will help you up."

I hesitated.

"Do you trust me?"

Nathan blew through his lips. Samuel shushed him.

Once again, I was the only one late for this party. I made my decision. "I trust you." I climbed onto the trunk and balanced there. He and Nathan circled, then edged close to me.

Samuel leaned down, his arm outstretched, his palm open. "Take my hand."

"What if I can't do this?" I was terrible with heights, and not all that great with taking chances.

In the near distance a man said, "What kind of guard are you, Daniel? It appears this gate is not properly closed."

"Now," Samuel insisted, his fingers reaching for and grazing my own.

I grabbed his hand, took a leap of faith and jumped toward him. He pulled me onto Nathan's back, and I landed directly behind him. I was fine. I was okay. In one piece—not broken.

"I knew you could do it," he said.

"Well then you have more faith in me than I do."

"Maybe it is time for you to have faith in yourself." He nudged Nathan with his knee. I clutched his waist tightly. We rode off slow and quiet at first, until we passed hearing distance from the garrison's walls.

Honestly I couldn't see much. It was dark and I held onto Samuel, my arms wrapped around his waist. We weren't in the cornfields. We seemed to be heading toward the ocean. I smelled salt air. Heard the crashing of the ocean waves on the Atlantic shore in the distance. I hadn't been on a horse since the day of our accident. The day Mama disappeared. This was terrifying. This was exhilarating.

"Ready?" Samuel asked.

My cheek rested against his back. I couldn't believe I was this high up in the air, still alive, and not having a panic attack. "Yes," I said.

"Good," Samuel said. "We do not have much time." He leaned forward, and murmured into Nathan's ear. He broke into a cantor and then a gallop. I hugged Samuel as hard as I could. We flew across the land, Nathan carrying us to our destination.

The wind whipped my face, and pushed my white cap off my head. My hair flew free behind me. "Do we have to go this fast?" I asked as my eyes teared from the wind.

"Yes," he said. "Why?"

"If I fall, I'd die," I said. "If I live, I'm in heaven." I decided to put my fears on hold for the moment. I'd let God, the universe, and that inner voice that guides each and every one of us, just have at it. But, I still clung to Samuel for dear life.

We survived our crazy run, arrived at our mysterious destination, a place close to the ocean. Nearby the waves slapped the sand and shoreline. What were we doing out here in the wilderness in the night, under a thick cloud cover that only specks of moonlight peeked through?

Samuel dismounted. Held my waist and lifted me off Nathan. I wobbled a bit when my feet landed on the earth. He steadied me, his hands on my shoulders.

"I'm good," I said.

"You are better than good," he replied. "You will get used to this."

"Get used to what?" I asked. *Breaking out of prison otherwise known as the garrison? Racing across a wild land in the dark of night, on the back of a beautiful horse? Holding tightly to the most honest, and handsome guy I'd ever met?*

"Traveling," he said. "Traveling quickly and without advance warning."

Oh. Got it. We were out here so he could teach me to time travel. More mentoring. More lessons. What was I thinking? He just wanted to be nice, and helpful, and help me heal. Daniel basically stated that when we snuck out through the gates.

"Are you thirsty?" he asked

I shook my head. "I'm fine," I said. *I'm in shock,* I thought.

Samuel gave Nathan some water from a flask he had packed. I thought he would tie him to a tree. But he rubbed his neck, whispered into his ear, and let Nathan wander, untethered. He trusted that the horse was so attached to him, that he would not leave us.

I wished I had the confidence that Samuel had.

He walked a couple of yards away from me, placed a blanket on the ground, and sat on it. "Come here."

"Isn't it super dangerous to be out here?"

"Yes. But, I need to show you something." He patted the blanket.

I sat down next to him. My teeth were chattering, and I shivered. Maybe it was the cold, maybe just all my adrenaline. "This better be great."

"It is better than great." He reached behind him, grabbed another blanket, and wrapped it around both our shoulders.

Our arms touched, as we sat, leaning into each other. It felt natural to be with him. It felt normal to lean my head on his shoulder. Strands of my hair blew across my face, and he tucked them back behind my ears. That felt delicious.

Maybe someday I would learn to become a Messenger. But right now, I wished on all the stars hidden up behind the clouds that covered the sky, and every Sa-Ta-Na-Ma chant ever said, that Samuel and I could be together. For real.

CHAPTER 22

Samuel spoke quietly. "I barely knew you before the Endicott attack, when you were just Abigail. You always acted superior, aloof. After the attack, you were confused, but you were funny and smart. You had a different frown."

Samuel noticed my frown. (*Note to self: sign up for charm school upon returning to the future.*)

"Your smile was different. A little crooked. Your entire being glowed...how can I say this...brighter? The more time I spent with you, the more my feelings changed. I knew something had changed. I was beyond curious. I needed to know more."

Just get on with it, I thought. Tell me the next thing I have to practice, or say, or do, or attempt to become a Messenger. Don't flirt. *Please don't mess with my heart.*

"Then, you told me your name was Madeline, that you lived in a place called Chicago many years in the future. And your life sounded bright, shiny, fast moving, and magical. To my dismay, I realized I had nothing to offer you."

"But that's not—" I began.

He put one finger to my lips. "Hear me."

I nodded, my heart pounding wildly.

"I spoke to Angeni about my feelings for you, and how exciting your real world must be, compared to here. I talked to a friend. I asked both for advice." He stood up and paced in front of me. "They told me I should just be myself with you. Show you whoever I was: good, bad, light and dark, strong, weak. That you would see me or not. And, then we could decide. If we were meant to be together, it would come from honesty and maybe a bit of magic. Just like the Sa-Ta-Na-Ma chant. Infinity chasing life, death, and rebirth."

His face was beautiful, his lips were full, his eyes intense. How could I get involved with a guy from the year 1675? But it was Samuel. How could I not? "Oh," I said.

"We are here, outside the garrison's safety because I wanted…no, I *needed* to show you part of who I am, and where I come from. Look." He pointed in front of us.

A slice of soft pink crept up on the horizon ahead. Funny, 'cause it had been so dark, I didn't even realize we were facing the horizon. The softness expanded into a deep rose; a sliver of dawn's sunrise rose from the night's blackness, and poked through the low, spotty, gray clouds. The rose blossomed into shades of fuchsia, accented with lemon yellows, oranges, and topped with blood reds.

Samuel had brought me here, and positioned us on the bluffs directly overlooking the Atlantic Ocean. There was no pollution, no planes or their trails in the sky. I was watching the most amazing, brilliant, pure sunrise I'd ever seen. It was stunning. Like how God/Goddess created the world before we all screwed it up with our crazy technologies.

"My people, the Wampanoag tribe are called The Children of the Morning Light," Samuel said. "We were here for thousands of years, and witnessed this sunrise every day, before anyone else came to these shores. This is I, Madeline. This is my truth."

I didn't know what to say to him. Had no idea what to do. This had never happened to me before. I felt like I was falling. But, for once, falling was a good thing.

"You come from a world where things glitter, shine, and move faster than I can imagine," Samuel said. "I want you to have something special—from this time. Something just for you, no matter how long you stay here." He held out his hand to me.

I touched his hand. His was steady. Mine shook. Perhaps from anxiety or the tension of holding so tight to him on our ride. The blood beat through our hands, and synchronized into one big pulse, like they were puzzle pieces meant to fit together. It felt mesmerizing. *It felt like I was coming home.*

"I made this for you. I hope you like it," he said. "And, if we are both lucky, maybe if, or when, you leave and go back to your world, you will find a way to take a piece of it with you."

What if I didn't want to go back to my world? What if I wanted to stay with Samuel, no matter what, or where, or when? But, if I never returned, it would kill Dad. Just like losing Mama almost killed him. And that would break my heart, as well.

I looked up at Samuel, and I swore the sunrise made his hazel eyes glint, and his black-brown hair gleam. Be still my flippin' heart. I peeled back the fingers on his fist. And saw the most beautiful gift cradled in his palm.

It was a necklace made from small, colorful feathers, long, coarse, black horsehairs and tiny purple and white seashells. It was exquisite. No one had ever made me a piece of jewelry before.

I picked it up from Samuel's hand, and dangled it over my head. The dawn's light reflecting off the ocean's waters shone through it. Each shell shimmered a different color. Together they turned into the most, glorious rainbow.

"Oh," I said, and ran my fingers over it. I felt my cheeks flush. "Oh. It's the most beautiful thing I have ever seen."

"Please?" He held his hand out.

I nodded.

He took the necklace, and slipped it over my head. It draped around my neck and down onto my chest. It felt like a piece of magic rested on top of my heart that beat so quickly. "Thank you." I gazed up at him.

He smiled, leaned his head down, and cradled my face in his rough palms. He pulled me to him and said, "Madeline. I do not care where you are from—the future, the past, a star in the sky. I will love you here now. I do not care what people think. I will love you in the past. I will love you in the future. I will love you, forever, Madeline."

And he kissed me.

I'd never felt a kiss like this. It was pure. It was sexy. It was honest. It was fierce. It was consuming. And I knew; this was it. There would never be another guy for me. I had traveled 300 plus years back in time and fallen completely in love with one soul. Samuel.

He finally stopped kissing me. "What are you doing?" I asked, almost breathless.

He smiled, and held out his hand to me. "We have to get back. Before they discover that we are missing."

"Are you sure?" *A kiss like that certainly needed to continue for a couple of hours, at the least.*

"We are destiny's lovers. If there is not time for us," he said as he took my hand, "then there will never be time for anyone."

CHAPTER 23

everal days passed. I did not see Samuel again.
Nothing had changed, but *everything* had changed.
For the first time in my life, I was in love. Not a crush, not
unreciprocated affections—like Brett. I was completely in
love. But my brain could not process both bliss as well as
confusion.

The elephant in the room was the fact I came from the
future. He lived in 1675. I was training to be a Messenger. He
was meant to be a Healer. And then there was the time travel
dilemma. Was there a way for us to be together?

I decided to ignore all the messy stuff, and just stick with
bliss. It had been a long time since I felt bliss.

I hummed my favorite Pink song as I helped Elizabeth
with the household chores and felt Samuel's necklace pressed
under my dress. I swept the floors. The necklace lay against
the skin of my neck and throat. The sensation was crazy. It
was silky, but coarse. Smooth, but rough. It was intoxicating.

I brought in wood and stacked the logs into the pile next
to the fireplace. The feathers tickled a little. I folded laundry
and replayed in my head what Samuel's face looked like as

the sun rose over the Atlantic. When he gave me the necklace. When he kissed me.

Elizabeth watched me from her chair close to the fireplace. "Something put a glow on your face," she said.

Oh yes. I smiled back at her.

The school kids sat close to her on small, wooden benches and clutched their odd hornbooks, practicing their letters on them.

When a loud, jolting knock slammed our front door, the kids jumped. Elizabeth's hand flew to her stomach and her face froze into a mask of terror.

"What?" I whispered.

"This is how they tell families their loved ones have been killed in the war," she whispered, sunk into her chair, and closed her eyes.

"Whoever it is I'll handle this," I said.

The kids were jumpy. Unspoken questions practically tripping off their tongues. "You have all been so smart today, children, that you get to take recess for a half hour."

They didn't budge, just stared at me, confused. I realized the word "recess" hadn't been coined yet. "Leave your books here." I pointed to their benches. "Go outside and run around. It's good for the blood."

"Yay!" A couple of kids popped off the benches, while the slower ones followed on their heels. Another harsh knock practically shook the house. The kids stopped in their tracks, and a few cowered.

Elizabeth started rocking. "No, Jebediah. Walk this earth with me. Be alive, I pray." She hunched forward, and clutched her huge belly.

I waved my hands in the air in front of the kids and whispered, "Hey!" I stuck out my tongue, crossed my eyes, and pulled on my ears. "Now who's scarier? Me or the person knocking?"

Two of them bent over, giggling.

"I'm going to open this door, and you run right past the person who's standing at the front door. But don't stray from Mistress Elizabeth's yard. Got it?"

"Got it," Mary Smythe said.

"I'm appointing you General, Mary. It's your job to make sure everyone who leaves this school house, comes back in." I saluted her.

Her eyes grew huge and she saluted me back.

A boy next to her pouted, "Since when do girls get to be Generals?"

"Since right now, smarty-pants." I opened the door and saw Reverend Wilkins leaning in for another knock. "Run, kids!" They ducked around him, and tore outside. The Reverend frowned and looked about as thrilled as someone who just got pelted with worms. "Good day Reverend Wilkins," I said. "Won't you come in?"

He pushed past me into the room. The cold, damp air from the gloomy fall day poured past him into our small home. He didn't even look at me, just stomped toward Elizabeth hunched over in the chair next to the fire. "Mistress Elizabeth Ballard."

She nodded and wiped a few tears away, but couldn't meet his eyes. I checked the kids playing in the dirt and yellow grass in front of the house. They seemed fine. I shut the door, walked to Elizabeth, and placed my hand on her shoulder. "Yes, Reverend?" I asked.

Again, he ignored me. "Mistress Elizabeth Ballard, wife of General Jebediah Ballard. We have a terrible situation."

Could this guy get more awful? Elizabeth reached her hand up to mine; it was trembling and cold. I leaned toward her, and whispered, "Be strong, Lizzie."

She nodded and looked up at him. "What is the situation, Reverend?" she asked. "Can it be resolved?"

"The situation rests squarely with your cousin, Abigail." He glared at me. "I am not sure we can solve it."

Elizabeth inhaled. "Jebediah is alive?"

"I believe so."

Thank God, I thought. And then I felt furious. How dare he frighten Elizabeth? He knew she'd be scared out of her mind that Jebediah had been killed.

He paced around me like I was some wild animal he was trying to capture; definitely not a puzzle piece he tried to figure out.

Elizabeth sat up straight. "Abigail heals from her wounds and helps me with the household chores. She keeps the children obedient." She pushed herself to standing. "What could possibly be wrong with her?"

The Reverend leaned his skinny face with his greasy hair into mine. He smelled rancid, like something left too long in the fridge, and I tried not to recoil. He latched onto the neckline of my dress, bunched it in his grimy fist, and ripped it. I cried out.

"Just as I was told," he said breathing heavily. He grabbed my necklace, yanked it from my neck, and squeezed it in his hand.

Elizabeth practically fainted. "What are you doing, Reverend?"

"That's mine!" I yelled. "You give it back!"

"Who are you really, Abigail?" He leaned into my face, his yellow teeth bared. "Because no God-fearing, colonial girl wears dirty, heathen jewelry."

I glared at him, which was like looking into the eyes of a rat up close. "A friend gave me this necklace," I said. "You have no right to take it. I ask you kindly to return my gift now."

"Ever since the attack you have turned into a tormented devil girl. Tell me truthfully. Are you one of Philip's spies?"

"Oh, please," I said. "Give my necklace back, or I'll take it back."

"Abigail!" Elizabeth exclaimed.

The Reverend dangled the most, beautiful piece of jewelry high in the air in front of me. I reached for it, but he ripped it apart. I watched, shocked, as crushed shells, pieces of Nathan's mane and broken feathers fell to the floor. My heart cracked into a million pieces as he destroyed the gift that Samuel had made, just for me.

"Oh no." Elizabeth crouched awkwardly, and gathered pieces of my necklace that lay scattered on the ground. "Apologize to the Reverend, Abigail."

"What!"

He smiled. "I counsel you to get control of your cousin. If something of this nature happens again, I will make sure she is punished as well." He sneered at me and strode toward the door.

I lunged at him, and grabbed his sleeve. "You pretend to be smart and God-fearing. But I know who you really are. At the end of the day, you're simply a bully."

Reverend Wilkins smiled at me with his tiny, yellow teeth. I pulled back, and really looked at him. Same teeth, same eyes, same bullying tactics, just three hundred plus years in time. But it was definitely he: *Stanley Preston.*

"Stocks and whipping would not be pleasant. But, you will soon discover that for yourself." He pushed past me and left.

"What did he mean?" I asked.

Elizabeth cradled her stomach and would not meet my eye. "As long as Jebediah is gone and we are at war, the Reverend Wilkins has the authority—"

I grabbed my coat from the rack, and flung open the front door. The kids ran back inside, their faces flushed from the cold.

"Be careful and prudent," Elizabeth hollered after me. "The Reverend has a reasonable point. I am sorry."

"I can't believe you'd take his side," I said. "I hate it here! You people are awful. I hope I never see you, ever again!"

"You do not mean that!" Elizabeth said.

I slammed the door behind me.

CHAPTER 24

*T*raced through the garrison and passed the church. I wondered if the Reverend was holed up there. I contemplated storming inside, and grabbing what was left of my necklace. Who had told him about it? Why? I had to find Samuel; I had to talk with him.

There was a small, tight crowd of people huddled together around the stocks and the hanging platform. I spotted Mistress Powter on the outskirts. She and her friends chatted to each other cheerfully, and pointed to the crowd's center. She beckoned to me, friendly. "Join us, Abigail. Hurry! You have almost missed it."

"Missed what?" I detoured from my path and with open arms they gathered and included me in their company.

"The punishment." Mistress Powter pushed me forward to the front of their group, and I saw who was being punished.

Samuel was shirtless. His hands were tied high to the whipping pole, while a colonist cracked a whip across his bare back that was already raw in areas and welting in others.

"No!" I cried out.

"Yes," Mistress Powter replied. "The Reverend Wilkins declared Samuel is guilty of lewd and unseemly behavior. Punishment is thirty lashes. And, to think you almost missed it." She craned her neck to catch a better glimpse.

Samuel caught my eye. "Go," he mouthed.

I teared up, and shook my head. "No!"

"Go." Another blow tore into his back, and he grimaced.

Reverend Wilkins spotted me and smiled. "So glad you could join us. *Abigail.*"

I pushed my way back through the small crowd, and ran toward Angeni's hut, wiping tears away with every step. I no longer cared if what I was living and feeling was a dream, a past-life, or real. It was time to go home.

I would learn from Angeni. I would get dizzy, climb tall things, and venture onto cliffs. I had to go back to my life in Chicago in the future. There was no way I would allow Samuel to ever be hurt again, because of me.

I leaned my head against her hut's coverings, listened, but heard nothing. "Angeni?" I whispered. There was no reply. I was bursting, and had to talk with somebody who would understand. Who would get it?

Tobias.

I walked the short distance to the garrison's walls. Saw long, black hair resting on the tall, muscular, and clothed back of a guy seated next to a flaming fire pit.

Tobias swiveled and faced me. Almost if he knew I was coming. He skinned what appeared to be freshly killed rabbits with his knife.

"Do you know what they are doing?"

"Yes," he said.

"Can't you stop them?" I begged.

"No."

"Why aren't you there for him? He's your best friend."

"He did not want me there," Tobias replied. "He did not want Angeni, or you there, either. He made me swear not to tell you in advance."

"Why would they hurt him?"

"Because they can." Tobias frowned. "Anyone can hurt anybody, and get away with it. Especially if they have cunning, skill, or power."

He was right.

"But how do I fight that?" I asked. "I can't live here knowing they are hurting Samuel, because of me."

Tobias skewered the rabbits' bodies with skinny, metal rods. "They have the power right now. Samuel and my kind do not. But power shifts with the winds. Ebbs and flows like the ocean waters. Today's friend becomes tomorrow's enemy. And history is written by the victors."

He slapped the rabbit carcasses on the rudimentary grill over the fire. "Sometimes I think history needs to be re-written. What do you think?" he glared at me.

"I think this garrison isn't my home," I said. "I have to leave, before people I care about get hurt, or even worse—are punished because of me."

"You never paid me back for the information I shared," he said, and stirred a pot that rested on the grill.

Really? That mattered now? "Fine. Ask me anything."

"What is your real name?" He pulled something from his pocket and sprinkled it into the pot.

I hesitated, but it was time. "Madeline Abigail Blackford."

"What are you doing living in Abigail Endicott's body and life?"

Great question. "I don't know."

"Where are you from?" he asked, took the pot off the stove and poured water from a flask into it.

"Chicago, Illinois."

"What year?"

"Over three hundred years in the future."

His face twitched.

"Do you think I'm crazy?"

"No," he said. "I think you might be a Messenger."

"What if I'm a Messenger who wants to go back to my time, and my people? Angeni says I can go back if I learn the Sa-Ta-Na-Ma chant, and confront my fears."

He shook his head. "You don't need to learn that old chant. There are other ways to travel."

"You know? Show me."

"You are not serious about leaving," he said. "You are just being whimsical, and leading everyone on a selfish chase."

"I want to go home."

"I think you want to stay here a bit longer. You are making friends, learning lessons. Even conquering hearts."

"I can't let Samuel get hurt again. Please, please help me."

"It tastes a little bitter," he said, and held out a metallic cup filled with brown liquid. "Drink it down quickly."

I looked at it. I really didn't like ingesting things when I wasn't sure about their contents. "What is it?"

He pulled the cup away, but I grabbed it back and gulped it down. Fine. Tobias was Samuel's friend. He only wanted what was best for him. Everything would be just fine.

It was worse than bitter. It tasted vile. It was all I could do not to spit it out. "How do you know about traveling? Did Angeni teach you?"

"No." He took the cup back from me and pulled the rabbit skewers from the fire. "My father knows about traveling," he said. "Sometimes when he hunts, he runs into a traveler."

"What'd ya mean?" I felt a little woozy and swayed. I sat down next to him.

"My father says traveling is filled with danger. Every time you travel becomes increasingly treacherous, as you meet more enemies the more trips you take." He stood up.

154

Well hopefully, I'd travel right back to my, wait, where was I going? "Where's Samuel? I need to say goodbye to Samuel before I leave." I tried to push myself to standing, but my legs felt like Jello and I sat back down.

"Recovering from being punished. Because of you."

"I'm sorry."

"Too late for sorry," he said. "You just stay here, relax, and enjoy your trip. If we're lucky, you'll be back with your real family in no time."

I was so dizzy. The fire seemed to be growing bigger. Just like the fire that consumed the cabin the first day I woke up here. That's when the skinned, crispy rabbits leapt off their skewers and hopped away.

Some jumped across the earth. Others disappeared into softball-sized holes in the ground that suddenly opened up around me with little gasps, like when you opened an airtight jar for the first time. My throat felt parched, and my stomach started cramping. "Don't go," I said.

He leaned into my face: all three, blurry versions of him. "You said you wanted to go back to your real life. I am helping you do that," Tobias said. "Go on now, Madeline. Be brave. Real Messengers are usually brave."

"But what 'bout Samuel?"

"I'll tell Samuel you said goodbye."

CHAPTER 25

I was alone in front of a fire with its flames licking at my feet, when a huge, loud blast of scorching air exploded in front of my eyes, sucked me inside and thrust me into its deepest interior: freezing darkness. I twirled around like a rag doll in this vacuum that was penetrated by pinpricks of multi-colored lights and images that popped up all around me.

Green from the pine needles in the forest where we hunted for herbs. Pink like the Atlantic sunrise. Purple like the shells in my necklace. Hazel like Samuel's eyes. Red like the welts on his back when he was whipped.

I heard snippets of conversations and saw people's faces. *Bam.* Mama. She threw me a kiss. "Life goes fast, Madeline. Right now we need to be just like life." *Poof*—she dissolved in pinpricks of light-like fireworks.

Bam. Samuel. "I love you, Madeline," he said as he gave me the necklace. It broke into pieces that morphed into fish-hooks, snagged parts of his beautiful face, and pulled it apart in different directions.

Bam. Tobias flew around me. "Give me something in

return." His face puffed out and morphed into a rattlesnake's head. A rattlesnake that appeared ready to strike.

I screamed.

"Just like you promised," Snake Tobias said, his tongue flitting in and out of his mouth while his body coiled. His snakehead and neck undulated, and then lunged like lightning toward me.

I threw myself backward, landed on my butt, and backpedaled as fast as I could away from him. I had no idea where I was. There was a dilapidated, rickety, wooden gate not too far ahead of me. I flipped over onto my stomach and crawled toward it as the snake—fangs bared—slithered toward me.

I reached it and shook it, hard. But it wouldn't open. "Hello!" I hollered. "I need help. Someone help me, please." Something slid across my foot, and I jumped. The snake wrapped itself around my ankle, and circled up my leg. I screamed again.

Help didn't seem to be coming, so I flung myself at the gate, and crashed through it. And just like that, I was standing in the doorway that led to my family's kitchen, in my real life.

Holy smokes. *I was back!*

My seven-year-old half sister Jane picked all the vegetables out of her omelet and methodically pushed them to the side of her plate.

"Eat your veggies, Jane," Sophie said.

"No," she said.

I brushed fire smudges and dirt from my face. Raked my fingers through my hair. And checked out my leg. No snake. Definitely no snake. I walked into our kitchen.

"Hey," I said. Like, I'd never been gone. Like, life was normal.

"Vegetables will help you grow healthy and live a long life," Sophie said.

"Don't think so," Jane replied.

"Eat half the green stuff, and we'll call it a day." Dad looked at his watch.

Squee! I was definitely home. I was back with my family. I never appreciated them until we were separated.

"I missed you guys like crazy," I said. "I love you all so much. I'm sorry I didn't say it before. Where's my omelet? Oh, you wouldn't *believe* what I was dreaming."

I looked around the table. There were place settings for three people. Not four. There were three chairs. One occupied by Dad, one by Sophie, and one by Jane. A fourth chair sat in the corner of the kitchen; a wilted plant plopped on it.

"I hate broccoli," Jane said. "And, I won't eat it."

Dad and Sophie shared a look.

"Hey," I said. "Jane's always been a picky eater. She hates broccoli, carrots, and anything that could possibly be in a salad. Why does this surprise you?"

Sophie pushed back her chair, got up, and grabbed Jane's plate. She took it to the kitchen sink, and rinsed it off. "You're going to the babysitter's." She opened the dishwasher, stuck the plate in the rack, and closed it.

"Do I have to? I want to go see Madeline."

"You already said goodbye to Madeline, sweetie. We talked about how Madeline might be going to live with her mama, today, in heaven."

What?

"No!" Jane pushed back her chair, and stormed out of the kitchen.

Dad leaned his elbows on the table and collapsed his head into his hands.

158

"Hello!" I hollered, and jumped up and down in front of my dad. "I'm back. I'm here!"

He got up off his chair and walked through me.

I shuddered.

He wrapped his hands around Sophie's waist. She had a small baby bump. "Taking Madeline off life support is the toughest decision we've ever made," he whispered.

Take me off life support?

Dad wiped a tear from his eye. "I just don't think she's going to make it. After all she's been through—she's not the toughest kid in the world."

"Maybe she will." Sophie wiped away a few tears of her own. "I told my office no more trips, until a year after our baby's born. They agreed. I keep full salary. I just don't travel."

"I love you." Dad kissed Sophie gently. "I'm going to get a few of Maddie's favorite things." He left the room.

"Sophie!" I cried. "Don't do this." I stood directly in front of her, inches from her face. "Please. I'm here. Really, I am." I waved my hands in front of her. Patted her cheeks with my hands.

Sophie leaned back against the kitchen sink and rubbed her stomach. Just like Elizabeth used to do. She closed her eyes, and tilted her face toward the heavens. "I miss you Madeline," she said. "I miss your spirit and how funny you are. I miss everything you bring to this family. I wish I could say I'd be okay with you dying. But honestly—I'm not. So, when the doctors disconnect you today, I want you to fight. I want you to stay alive. Do you hear me? Fight, Madeline."

The thing was? I'd never been much of a fighter.

———

I blinked, and the next thing I knew I lay in a field filled with wildflowers. I gazed up at the pretty blue sky spotted with a few white clouds that danced across it. I remember this field, because Mama and I had danced here before, spinning in circles and giggling like we shared the funniest joke.

A soft, mechanical, rhythmic noise that sounded like a complete breath—a long slow inhale and a low exhale— hummed in the background. That is—if a machine could breathe.

I stretched my arms over my head. Even though I was still in my colonial clothes, I felt happy, light, almost giddy. Then I saw the strangest thing: the dead colonists from the Endicott settlement were alive and healthy, walking past me, and going about their outdoor work. They carried buckets and shovels. Maybe they were gardening.

"Hello," I said to the young colonial women whose neck had been caked in blood the first time I saw her. Her neck was now perfect: long, thin, and completely intact. "I remember you."

She smiled at me shyly, and placed two buckets of dirt next to me. "It is very exciting, yes?"

"What's exciting?" I asked.

The guy who had the hideous burns on his arm, walked past me healthy and unscathed. He carried a shovel and winked at me. "The news that you get to be with your soul mate, for an eternity," he said.

"I get to be with Samuel, forever?" Feeling giddy morphed into feeling euphoric. I didn't even care when the colonists from the Endicott settlement dug their shovels into the buckets of dirt and pitched soil onto my body.

Because I got to be with Samuel—forever.

The soft, rhythmic, machine-breathing sounds stopped.

And, I drifted. I was maybe fifty feet up in the air looking down at my very still, white face, my body wearing a colonial dress, covered in dirt. I could hear everything; see every-

THE MESSENGER

thing. The colonists seem satisfied, and walked off. Except for the girl.

She placed a few sprigs of lavender and sage on my chest, kissed my cheek, and whispered into my ear, "It is not over, yet. You can still fight. Only if you want. I did not get that chance."

She left. I lay on that field filled with wildflowers. I smelled burnt sage, lavender, and freshly baked, chocolate chip cookies. It felt like it was time to finally be free. When something white, small, and feathery dove through the air past me toward the earth.

A small white bird fluttered next to my body. *What was this thing doing?* Didn't matter. I was out of here. That's when I felt a pinch on my leg. This stupid bird was pecking me.

It jabbed my thigh. Nipped my ankle. "You'd better flippin' stop it!" I said, when suddenly I was sucked from the skies back into my body on the ground.

The bird hovered over me, dived, and pecked my arm. "Ouch!" I fought it off, my arms flailing. I think I nailed it as it stopped pestering me for a few seconds. Then, that dang bird dove in and pecked my ear.

"Madeline!" Samuel whispered. But his voice was so far away. I bolted upright, brushed the dirt off me, and looked around the meadow. It was beautiful. But something was wrong: I wasn't breathing.

Stupid anxiety. I should probably breathe. I inhaled. *Ouch.* My lungs felt like they were glued together. I exhaled and took another breath. This time it felt like my lungs were ripping open.

I heard a woman's voice chant, "Sa. Ta. Na. Ma. Sa. Ta. Na. Ma."

The earth tipped underneath me, and I was falling. *My biggest fear.* I grabbed onto the flowers but they slid through my fingers. I clawed the earth, as the rest of my body seemed to be caught up in some kind of insane wind, blowing me like a speck of dust in a storm.

Angeni said, "Let go."

The earth turned again. Now the land was over my head, and my legs dangled into a dark abyss. I hung on with all my strength as the winds buffeted me.

"I'm scared!"

"Let go."

Really. What did I have to lose at this point?

I let go.

I dropped from the earth above me, fell through the winds that whirled around me, and catapulted past the colonial people watching me from the sidelines. The nice girl smiled and clapped her hands.

I heard Pachelbel's Canon play as I fell through a rainbow of colors in a gorgeous, Atlantic sunrise, and saw the sandy beach coming up far too quickly. I was going to hit hard. Really hard. I squeezed my eyes shut.

CHAPTER 26

I touched down on the ground, soft as a feather.

My eyes fluttered open. "Sa. Ta. Na. Ma." Angeni twirled next to me in her tiny, dark hut. I lay on the floor. I felt something light and ticklish on my chest, reached for it, and felt feathers, bones. I lifted Angeni's gorgeous necklace up in the air. It reminded me of the bird, but that wasn't possible.

Angeni stopped twirling, sighed, and took her necklace from me. "You are back." She stroked my cheek. "Why did you take the dark medicine?"

"What's the dark medicine?" I rubbed my head. "Is this what a hangover feels like?"

"No. It is what nearly dying from poison feels like," Angeni said. "You traveled. But you did it with poison, and it almost killed you. If you travel with the dark medicine, and do not return, you vanish. Forever. No infinity. No re-birth. Bringing you back this time was much more difficult than the other times. Do not do this again." She frowned and tucked her necklace away under the bench with the furs on top.

"But I was worried about Samuel and—"

"And what? Decided to heap more anguish upon his soul, than he already experiences? He loves you. He knows this is a nearly impossible love. But Samuel loves purely."

I flashed to that awful sight of him being whipped. "Is he okay?"

"He will heal." She reached for her medicine bag. "Who gave you the dark medicine?"

"Oh. Um." If I told her that it was Tobias, he would not only get in trouble, but he would cause even more for me. I would deal with Tobias on my own. But not until my head stopped spinning, and my stomach felt less queasy.

"I think I already know who. The same person who told the Reverend about the necklace Samuel made for you." Angeni handed me some leaves. "Chew on these. They will help your stomach sickness."

"Tobias told the Reverend?" I asked.

She nodded. "Who else? Samuel only shared his feelings about you and making your totem necklace with Tobias and myself. The only people he trusts."

My totem necklace? Tobias had ratted us out to the Reverend knowing full well Samuel would be whipped?

Angeni kissed me on my cheek. "You are a good girl. Daniel will escort you to Elizabeth's home." She opened the skins to her hut, and there was Daniel, plain as day.

"You missed the courier!" Daniel exclaimed. "General Jebediah and our troops return tomorrow. There was a bloody battle. Not everyone survived. There are wounded."

"Then, there is much to prepare." Angeni pulled a fur pelt from under the bench and wrapped it around her shoulders. I spotted her necklace and some deerskin clothes.

"Where are you going?" I asked.

"A stubborn young man refuses to leave that horse. But he needs food and medicine. As well as news about you."

Daniel and I walked through the garrison. It wasn't night-time yet, but I guess Angeni wanted him to accompany me in case I pitched over dead. I asked him to tell me what it was like to guard the gates. That made him happy. He went into detailed explanation while I thought about my next step.

Telling the Reverend and destroying my necklace was awful. Maybe Tobias didn't think Samuel would be physically punished. After all, I wasn't. Maybe in all fairness, Tobias hadn't meant to poison me.

Maybe he just wanted me to travel. Leave this place, this time. Leave him, Samuel, and everyone else alone. But I didn't really believe that. I think Tobias was planning more evil. And I needed to know what that was.

Tomorrow the garrison would be filled with more people. There'd be increased commotion, but there would also be more eyes. There was no time. I realized what I had to do. And I had to do it tonight.

"That's fascinating, Daniel," I interrupted. Frankly, he could have been pontificating about hunchback whales, 'cause I'm not sure I heard a word he said. "We must go back to Angeni's. I forgot the, uh, blanket that she wanted me to give Elizabeth." The blanket that would hide everything I was going to borrow from Angeni.

Then, I had one more detour to check on Nathan. I knew he wouldn't be in the barn. But I needed to stash what I had borrowed in the pile of blankets that lay on the floor in the corner.

Once Elizabeth heard the news that her beloved Jebediah was alive and coming home, she finally relaxed. I waited until she slept soundly to sneak out of the house. I carried a small candle resting in a metal cup, and a tiny wooden bowl I'd filled with dirt.

I made my way quietly to the barn. Placed the candle on the ground far from anything that looked overtly flammable. I stripped off my dress, and dropped it onto the cold floor next to my feet. I wiggled out of the ridiculous undergarments, yanked the white cap from my hair, and tossed it on the heap of clothes.

I shivered and wondered; could I do this? I knew I was meant to be with one soul: Samuel. I was in love with him, and amazed he loved me in return—flaws and all.

I pulled on the buckskin breeches and tunic that I had borrowed from Angeni's hut. I tied a black rag around my head, and shoved my hair up underneath it. I saw Angeni's necklace lying on the floor, and I picked it up.

It was wild, and beautiful, and fierce. Exactly, how I needed to feel tonight. I knew it was Angeni's totem. Mine had been destroyed. Maybe, she wouldn't mind if I borrowed it—for just one night.

I draped it over my head and shoved Abigail's clothes behind a bale of hay. When I returned in a couple of hours, I'd change into that costume, and go back to being a proper colonial girl. Right now—I wasn't going to be all that proper.

I reached for the wooden bowl filled with the dark earth. Spat on my fingers and poked them into the clay. Pulled out dark chunks and rubbed them on my face, hands, and feet. I held up the candle in the metallic cup, and tried to view my reflection.

I didn't look anything like Abigail in 1675, or Madeline in my real life. I wasn't sure if I looked like a Messenger, a warrior, or a fool. Maybe all of them rolled into one person. Yeah. That sounded like me.

I still had anxiety, but I had to find out what Tobias was doing in the woods at night. What was he planning next? I could not let him hurt Samuel, ever again.

I took a deep breath, and squeezed out of the barn's door.

CHAPTER 27

I crouched barefoot against the side of the barn. A break in the thick cloud cover overhead revealed a new moon. I watched and waited for Tobias. It didn't take that long.

He walked silently along the fence's perimeter. How was he going to get past the guard? Daniel wasn't on duty tonight. Was the guard in on his plot as well?

Tobias dropped to his knees next to a squat, sawed-off tree trunk. He eyeballed the area, searching for anyone who might be watching. I doubted he even considered looking for me, the colonial girl with delusions. The girl his best friend had fallen for. The girl he had poisoned.

Tobias pushed the tree trunk aside and dropped into a hole in the earth underneath it. His hand reached up as he pulled the trunk back over the hole. I waited a few moments, and followed him. He was obviously on a mission.

So was I.

I crouched and ran, pulled the trunk aside, and dropped into the hole. I found myself in an earthen tunnel propped up with tree branches. I couldn't see its other end. I gritted my teeth, pulled the trunk back across its opening, and was in complete darkness.

I crawled on my stomach, pulling myself forward with my hands. I really hoped there weren't bugs down here. What if this thing gave way, and I was buried alive in dirt?

I crawled for possibly the longest minutes of my life 'till I saw whispers of moonlight peeking through what looked like a thicket of weeds and skinny branches.

I wriggled forward, peered out, and spotted Tobias far away in the distance. I waited a long moment then pushed on the branches. They gave way easily, and I pulled myself out onto solid ground.

I pursued Tobias from as far away as I possibly could, without losing sight of him. I had an idea where he was going.

He walked quickly on a narrow dirt path that rimmed brown, battered, dying corn fields, that were probably once filled with tall, fresh crops planted and tended to by the Indian women, and eventually farmed by colonial men.

Recently, these fields had been beaten down in a battle during King Philip's War. The bodies of the injured and dying men that fell here were both Native and colonists.

Despite the chilly weather, there was a reason I went barefoot. I didn't want the sound of clunky shoes to give me away. When I tripped over something abandoned in the field, flew forward, but managed to stay upright.

The thing I tripped over wasn't very big. It felt dense under my foot, a little gooey and crusty. The stench of rotting meat, with a pinch of sweetness hit my nostrils. I crouched to avoid keeling over. I peered at the thing I tripped on that lay right in front of me: it was dull and shiny all at the same time. I reached down, touched it, and rolled it over: it was the remains of a human arm.

I gagged and recoiled. I couldn't see if the color of the skin was dark or light. It didn't matter, because the sunlight would confirm this arm was gray, black, chewed on by animals, and devoured by insects. So much for societal differences and whose politics history had proven right.

Tobias headed toward the forest in the near distance. I knew it was crazy, and dangerous to be out here at night on my own, following a guy who hated me. Any moment, I could run into some of King Philip's warriors and be taken hostage—like that preacher's wife.

Most of the time, I was so far behind him, that I barely spotted his movements. Tracking and following him was far from easy. There were several times I thought I'd lost him for good, and wondered if I should give up my insane mission, and return to the safety of the garrison.

But then, the low clouds opened for spare moments, the moon shone, and I'd catch a glimpse of him far ahead of me. The chase was still on.

I followed Tobias for what seemed like an eternity, but was probably a little over a half hour. The wind picked up, the temperature plummeted, and I knew from living in Chicago that there was an early freeze on the way.

I wished I'd borrowed a fur wrap. By the time Tobias disappeared into the forest, I had to concentrate to keep my teeth from chattering, which would definitely blow my cover. I took a deep breath, and squeezed into its blackness.

Tracking Tobias in the woods was different from following him through the fields. The forest was darker, with towering fir and pine trees, leaves on the ground covering tree roots, and fallen branches which I could easily trip over.

Before taking each footstep, I thought what Samuel taught me: *walk with silence.* Let your feet sink into the earth with consciousness, and rise with lightness. *Be untraceable;* don't bend branches, or flatten the leaves on the ground in a pattern from your weight. But, I was no expert at this yet. I tread quietly over thick tree roots covered with leaves. When, I spotted him.

Tobias squatted next to an enormous boulder resting half in a pond's waters, and half on its shore.

I ducked behind a large tree trunk, and pushed one hand onto my chest, trying to force my anxious heart to still. I swear it pounded like ceremonial drums. I silently prayed 'Please God, make my heart stop beating so flippin' loudly before it gives me away.'

Tobias's head swiveled in my direction. Did he see me? If so my spy days were over. He'd race to my side and confront me. I didn't think we'd politely discuss why I was following him. Especially not with me wearing a Native American, Rambo-esque disguise.

The moon flitted out from under the clouds, and the sounds of the rushing river, and thundering cadence of the waterfall in the distance filled the forest. Tobias's eyes narrowed as he looked away from where I hid, surveyed the land around him, then tilted his head back, closed his eyes and I swear; he sniffed the air.

I heard an animal cry in the near distance, but suspected that the call was made by a human to signal Tobias. He jogged, skirting the edges of the pond and headed toward the cliffs that lay between the pond and the river leading to the waterfall. I struggled to breathe quietly.

Tobias ran into an opening in the rocks, that led to the caves; a perfect place to meet someone in secret.

I kept low to the ground, raced to the boulder, and crouched behind it. I would wait here. I leaned back against it, and my feet sunk into the wet, pebble-filled sand. A paper-thin layer of ice grew on the pond's surface.

The wind whipped up and howled as it ricocheted across the boulders. I don't know how many minutes passed. My cheeks and earlobes stung. I shivered, hugged myself, and realized my breath was now visible in short, smoky puffs in front of my face.

When someone grabbed me around the throat from behind, ripped the rag off my head, and latched onto my hair.

My neck whiplashed, and my head bounced back. I screamed, but a large, rough hand clamped over my mouth.

"Hello, Madeline," Tobias said.

CHAPTER 28

*J*tried to bite his hand, but he just pressed it harder against my face and yanked me backward across the pebble-studded beach. I tried to kick him. But my legs flailed, my feet bouncing off stones. Change of plans—I dug my heels into the sand, and shoved my elbow into his ribs.

"Oof!" He kept dragging me.

I slipped my foot around his, tripped him, and we crashed onto the wet sand. He landed on his back—hard. My fall was softer, as I landed almost completely on top of him. His grip on my hair, throat, and mouth relaxed for moments, and we lay face to face.

"Why do you hate me?" I asked.

"Because you, and your mama, ruin everything."

What did Mama have to do with any of this? I pushed myself off him, and spun around to make a run for it.

He grabbed Angeni's necklace, pulled it tight around my neck, and stopped me cold. "I'm going to kill you." He wrapped the necklace taut into a stranglehold. "And I will welcome the pleasure it brings me."

The shells bit into my skin, and I felt pinpricks of pain

from each tiny puncture wound. A very old and deep emotion shifted inside me. After all I'd been through, I was not ready to be a willing victim, a lamb to the slaughter.

In my head I heard Sophie say, "I want you to fight. I want you to stay alive. Do you hear me? Fight, Madeline."

"Not without a fight," I said, head butted him, and bit his ear, hard.

Tobias grunted in pain, but didn't release his hold on the necklace. Our faces locked together like pieces of a jigsaw puzzle that were carved perfectly, made to fit into each other.

We tumbled across the rough, rocky sand onto the pond's sheer layer of ice. It sounded like thin glass shattering, as we broke through it and sank, face to face, kicking and pummeling each other.

Underwater, everything appeared blue and icy. Tobias pulled me deeper into its depths. I yanked one of my arms free and clawed his face. He recoiled, and I broke out of his headlock.

My lungs felt like they were going to explode. Air bubbles escaped my mouth, as I kicked my way to the pond's surface, splintered up through the ice, and rasped for breath. I pinwheeled my arms and legs in reverse and half swam, half crashed, away from him.

Tobias's head popped out of the pond's surface, ice slivers clinging to his thick neck. We treaded water, and glared at each other, just yards apart.

He panted and touched his bleeding ear. He looked like a dangerous wounded animal.

"I know you love Samuel," I said. "I do, too. In a different way." My feet made contact with the pond's bottom. Shivering, I dragged myself out of the water.

"You do not *know* Samuel. You could not *even dream* what this is about," he said.

I made it onto the pond's shoreline, pitched forward, and

collapsed in the sand. "And, you don't know anything about my mama. Don't include her in any grudge you have against me." Drenched, beat up, I watched him, wary, as he staggered out of the pond toward me.

"I know more about your mama than you ever will." His eyes were dilated.

I pushed myself to standing and stumbled away from him.

He pulled his rabbit-skinning knife from a sheath on his belt.

I backpedaled.

"We were there when you and your mama had the car accident," Tobias said.

"What?" I stopped and faced him. How could he know about that?

"We track you Messengers. We find where, and what year, you exist. Let's see. Madeline Abigail Blackford. Sixteen-years-old. Student, junior year at Preston Academy in Chicago. Your mama disappeared after a car accident ten years earlier. Who do you think caused that accident?"

"I don't know. They never found the person. Who are you?"

He laughed. "I am a Hunter. We make note of your pathetic Messenger lives. Keep track of how many times you've traveled and whom you deliver messages to. If you have changed anyone's life, well, then you get a little more attention from my people. If you upset the balance, disturb the world's equilibrium, or outlive your usefulness? *We destroy you.*"

"You're a freak," I hissed.

"No. I am practical. Unlike you, Madeline. You are a weak, un-schooled Messenger, who does not deserve to live one minute longer, in any life that you unwittingly traveled to."

Tobias raised his knife, and flung it with perfect aim toward my heart.

I gasped, heard my heart thump in my ears, the wind whistle, and I cringed as that knife flew through the air straight toward my chest.

There was a loud, angry roar.

Samuel leapt across the sand, wrapped his body around mine, and tackled me. We tumbled, rolling onto the sand. Tobias's knife skimmed over us, clunked against a large rock, and landed next to Samuel, who picked up the knife and glared at Tobias.

"You know, she does not belong here," Tobias said. "Does not need to exist in the future. The world will not miss her in any time period. She does not belong at all."

"You are wrong. She belongs with me," Samuel said. "No matter the year, no matter what spirit desires for us, *she will always belong with me.*"

"No! You and I will change the future," Tobias said. "Hunter and Healer. Two halves of a whole. Hunters take out those who are wounded. Not necessary. Beyond redemption. Healers create better lives for those who deserve to remain."

"That might have been your plan. But it was never mine. Your hatred, your fear, whatever this is. I loved you like a brother, Tobias. But this is over." Samuel hurled the knife toward Tobias.

I hid my face against Samuel's shoulder. Tobias cried out, grunted, and I heard him hit the ground hard. Samuel winced. His entire body tightened around me and seemed to contract for a moment.

"I am so sorry. So sorry," I cried.

"I am, too," Samuel said. "For everything."

I sobbed uncontrollably. For Tobias, as well as the life I left behind. And for Mama—because for the first time, I realized—she had never planned to leave me.

CHAPTER 29

*W*e didn't have time to dig a perfect grave for Tobias. We hauled large rocks, weighed his body down, and buried him in the pond. Samuel and I held hands as we each said one silent prayer for Tobias's soul. Then, we raced back to the garrison.

In the barn, I managed to dress in my colonial clothes and covered up the legion of bruises and punctures around my throat. But, I couldn't cover the body aches, and pains, and stiffness that were settling in from having to fight for my life. I shoved the wet skins under the blankets. But I couldn't find Angeni's necklace. Probably lying on the bottom of the pond.

Samuel hugged me lightly, kissed my forehead, and his lips brushed my bruised neck. "I never would have let him get close to you if I believed he was consumed with evil. This is my fault."

"No it's not. I knew something was wrong and followed him. Maybe if I left Tobias alone—everything would be just fine. Maybe if I never traveled here—everything would be normal," I said. "You and Tobias would still be best friends— hunting rabbits, sneaking out after dark, and exploring."

"Tobias wanted me to take his concoction and travel, but I refused. It did not feel right." Samuel shook his head. "I know that Angeni travels without potions or medicines. I have no idea how you traveled here. But if you had not? I would never have known it is possible to love this completely."

"What about Tobias? What do we do now? "

"We do nothing. We say nothing. There is nothing to be done. "I cannot lose you now, Madeline." Samuel caressed my head and neck. "Promise me, I will not lose you?" He wiped the tears from my face.

"I promise," I said. "You will not lose me. You will never lose me."

"Now, go. Hurry to Elizabeth's house," he said. "Do not look back at me in case someone spots you. But know I follow until you are safely home."

I slipped inside Elizabeth's house, went to my sleeping mat, and lay down. But I couldn't sleep. I tossed, and turned, and ruminated. Tobias was dead, because of me. Why did he want Samuel to travel? How did he know about Mama? Could his people really have caused our accident? Too many thoughts. Eventually my adrenaline crashed, and I dozed.

I smelled burnt sage, lavender and freshly baked chocolate chip cookies.

From the back seat, I could see the front of Mama's car jutted out over the guard wire. We hung high between the open-aired parking garage and the riverbank below it. I screamed.

"You're my good girl, Maddie," Mama said, her forehead sweaty and bloody as she wrangled the last lock that held me in the booster seat. "We're almost out of here." When, some monstrous vehicle rammed us again from behind. Our car lurched forward for a second time, and Mama fell backward into the driver's seat.

We hung nearly vertical, and I peered through our cracked windshield that distorted the view of the ground far below it.

Except for the creaking sounds our car made, everything else grew deathly quiet. A car door slammed behind us, and someone's heavy shoes clipped methodically on the concrete. A man said, "It's time, Rebecca."

"No! I will not travel this time. I will not abandon Madeline this way." Mama looked around frantically.

"You have to," the man said. "If you don't travel now, your combined weight will tip the car off the edge. You know how to stay alive. But Madeline doesn't. She won't survive falling ten stories. She will die, and you won't even be around to bury her."

He leaned out over the guardrail and waved at me though the crack in the window. "Hello, Madeline," he said. "I think I'd recognize you anywhere."

A thick chunky silver ring shone on his hand. I screamed. "Mama!"

She burst into tears, and shook her head. "No!"

The guy kicked the back of our car, and we teetered like a playground ride gone terribly wrong.

"It's your choice. Stay and know that you've killed your daughter. Or leave, and possibly live to fight another day."

Mama wiped the tears from her eyes. She reached over the seat, grabbed my hand, and said, "Life goes fast, Made-

line. Know in your heart that I never wanted to leave you."
She blew me a kiss, and then let go of my hand.

Leave me?

Mama opened the driver's door. That didn't look good.
There was nothing between the front seat and the ground
but air.

"Now, Rebecca," the guy said.

"Only if you promise to leave Madeline alone. Stay away
from her. Promise me."

"You know I do not make promises I cannot keep."

"Fine. Take us both, because I'll die with her. I will not
travel," Mama said.

"But you have to," the guy said. Except now he sounded
worried, his voice cracked. "We need your—"

"Expertise? Experience? Magic?" Mama asked. "Promise
me, Malachi, that you and your people will not lay a hand on
Madeline until she reaches the age."

The car creaked in the wind for what seemed like an
eternity.

"I promise you on Hunters' blood, that we will not touch
Madeline until she is of age. But only if you come with
us now."

Mama nodded. "It's done," she said, resigned. "Look at
me, Madeline."

I did.

"Listen for my voice. If you hear it, when you hear it,
please come to me." She looked me square in my eyes. "I love
you always, my darling daughter."

Mama stepped out of the car and hovered for seconds in
the air. Her face was pure, her eyes clear. Then she plummeted toward the earth, the wind blowing her long hair up
into the air.

The car immediately tilted back toward the parking
garage floor. The back wheels landed with a thud on the

floor. I heard the *clip, clip, clip* of the guy's shoes as he walked away from our car.

Someone in the garage hollered, "Oh my God! Call 911!"

"There's someone in the back seat of that car!"

"It's a kid!"

A small, white bird flew off into the sky, right where Mama had fallen. I realized I was alone, and I screamed again.

CHAPTER 30

*E*lizabeth jiggled my shoulders and woke me. I winced. Every piece of my body hurt. "Another bad dream?"

I nodded and struggled to be back in this world. Not the dream where I just remembered our entire car accident—and how Mama disappeared. She hadn't wanted to leave me. All these years, all my anger—it wasn't her fault.

"I am happy you returned yesterday. I know the Reverend Wilkins was harsh, and what he did to your necklace must have felt terrible. But he has to be strict. That is his job."

"He's an idiot." I patted my collar, making sure it was high on my neck, and she wouldn't spot the bruises. I could always say they were from the Reverend's violence, not Tobias.

"I made you porridge." She handed me the bowl and looked at me a little funny. "How did you get mud on your face?"

I shrugged. "I was at the barn for a bit yesterday. Are you feeling okay? How's the baby? Is Jebediah back yet?"

"The baby and I feel healthy." Elizabeth leaned toward me

and kissed me on my head. She pushed herself to standing and walked off. "Thanks to you. Do not forget we have special church services to welcome our men home from the war."

"Okay," I said. We both heard the sounds at the same time.

Yelling and hollering; foot stomping and cheering; crying and laughing. A few gunshots rang out. The troops were obviously home. The celebration had begun. But as quickly as the fireworks began, they disappeared. There was an uneasy quiet. Something didn't feel right.

Jebediah Ballard flung open the front door to the house, strode in, swept Elizabeth into his arms, and kissed her passionately. He pulled away, and placed his hand gently on her enormous belly.

"You are back. You are back!" Elizabeth burst into tears as I studied my feet, but managed to peek at them. No wonder she was taken with him. While Jebediah was obviously older than her by about fifteen years, he was handsome and in great physical shape.

"I missed you so much, Elizabeth. I thought of you every hour. Every day," Jebediah said. "How is our child?"

"Alive. Healthy." Elizabeth wiped her tears away. "We almost lost this child. But Angeni and Abigail helped save the both of us."

Jebediah backed away from Elizabeth and registered me. "You look different, Abigail." He eyeballed me.

"I have a scar."

"War wound," he said. "You are a relative. Call me Jebediah. Like you used to, before your unfortunate accident. I need you to sit, Elizabeth. I have disturbing news."

Elizabeth's face blanched. He held her hand as she awkwardly sat on the chair she used when the school kids were here.

"Who amongst our soldiers did not make it back?" she asked.

"Earnest Young and Raymond Forde were killed in battle. They died honorably."

"Oh," she said and collapsed her forehead into her hand, while her other hand clutched her heart.

"I know Raymond Forde was your suitor before we met," Jebediah said. "His loss will bring you pain."

"Yes, it will. But Raymond was never more than a true friend, Jebediah. Nothing more…"

Enough. I didn't know how much more drama Elizabeth could take right now. She was so close to having her baby. The last thing she needed was to go into early labor.

"Excuse me, Jebediah. I think—"

He waved me off, like I was a gnat. "That is not the worst," he said. "On our way home we passed the Big Rock Pond. The one by the caves."

"Yes, I know of it." She looked up at him, her face turning gray.

"We came upon a fresh body washed up on the shores."

My hands trembled.

"Another wartime casualty?" Elizabeth asked. "Someone we know?"

A lump grew in my throat and my breath turned raspy.

"The body was Tobias. As far as we can tell—it was not a battle. Someone murdered Malachi's son."

In my dream I watched Mama step out of our car, and drop toward the earth. A man named Malachi made her do that. I hyperventilated.

"Oh no! Malachi and Tobias were as close as a father and son could be," Elizabeth said. "He will be devastated." She wiped tears away. "Do you have any idea what happened? Who would do this?"

Jebediah nodded. "We found this tangled in Tobias's

184

clothing." He pulled Angeni's necklace from his pocket, and stuck it in front of Elizabeth's nose. "I know you care for Angeni. But she tracked and killed Tobias in a blatant act of revenge."

"No!" I cried.

"Do not push me, Abigail!" Jebediah spat. "I have heard all about your unholy relations with Samuel. You have strained everyone here to his or her breaking points. If inclined, I could have you arrested as well."

They arrested Angeni.

"No, Jebediah, no." Elizabeth took his hand. "Abigail saved our baby. It's a son. I know it. She saved our firstborn son."

"Really?" Jebediah smiled. "A son, you believe?"

I broke into a sweat, watched the walls close in on me, and stopped breathing. I launched into a full-blown panic attack.

Apparently, I lay on the floor for several hours, which felt like days, while Elizabeth applied cold cloths to my head. "It must be a touch of her head wounds," I heard her say multiple times.

When I recovered from my attack, and could sit up, Elizabeth told me that Jebediah had left the house. Apparently he, Reverend Wilkins, and Malachi were seeing to Tobias's burial. Angeni was already under arrest. They imprisoned her in a tiny cell, almost like an underground shed, attached to the church.

"How can they believe Angeni killed Tobias?" I asked. "She's nearly blind. There's no way she'd be able to track him to wherever that pond is."

"Everyone knows Angeni is magical. She is different. Jealous people have called her a witch. It is the necklace. That is really the only proof," Elizabeth said. "Are you feeling better?"

I didn't know what I was feeling anymore. Guilt. Enormous guilt. This was all my fault. I felt terror. Panic. Excruciating sadness. "What will they do to her?" I asked.

"They will try her. If found guilty, they will hang her," Elizabeth said.

"Will anyone testify for her?" I asked. "Will anyone come to her defense?"

She sighed. "No."

CHAPTER 31

*A*ngeni's trial was held the next day in the church. Seems the garrison's entire population had shown up, and there was a waiting line to get in. I caught my first glimpse of Malachi when the crowd parted for him to enter the building.

He was an older Native man. He was dark-skinned with a tuft of black hair adorned with three feathers sprouting from the top of his shaved head. He was lean, ripped, and had an athlete's body. His eyes were weathered, but knowing. His lips were thin and hard. He wore a thick, chunky, silver ring on his left hand, and was dressed in animal skins, not unlike those I wore the night I tracked Tobias.

After the jurors entered, the crowds pushed and shoved to get in to see the show. Despite Elizabeth's requests for me to stay away—I had to be there. I had to support Angeni. But, as I elbowed my way into the church, Daniel and one of his friends grabbed me, and yanked me back from the church steps.

"Hey!" I said.

Daniel replied. "If you are here, you will only make things

worse for everyone." They escorted, (aka, dragged) me back to Elizabeth's house where we waited. I didn't put up a fight, or try to escape. I knew that this time—they were right.

Daniel came and went throughout the trial, giving us updates. The news was passed from a person close to the church door to the people gathered outside because Angeni's trial was standing room only.

Three witnesses for the prosecution were called. One testified she had seen Angeni practicing black magic: summoning the demons and shape shifting into a wolf who ate colonial babies after they were born. That's why so many of the garrison's children died in infancy.

Another witness swore under oath, that Angeni was a spy for King Philip. She'd sneak into the woods at night and give Philip's liaison a full accounting of where the colonial troops would be, and how he could best attack them. Apparently, she was also a mind reader, and knew what the colonial generals were planning.

The last witness testified she once overheard Angeni talked about the future. Shiny fast-moving ways to travel. Tall buildings that rose almost one hundred stories into the air. But yet families still loved each other. Could you imagine that? Families still loved each other. *Another heinous crime.*

The Reverend Wilkins called for witnesses to speak on Angeni's behalf: no one came forward. Not one person whose fever she lowered, whose broken arm she set, whose child she saved from a dreaded infection.

The verdict was handed down within minutes following the testimony. Angeni was found guilty. The Reverend Wilkins sentenced her. She would be hanged the next day on the commons.

I lost it. I screamed and cried. Elizabeth tried to make me drink the medicinals, but I refused. To say I was in shock was an understatement. I had to find Samuel. I think Daniel and his friends had kept him out of sight as well. They did not want to fan the flames of this crowd's insane anger worse than it already was.

"Where is he?" I asked Daniel. He just shook his head. "Where is Samuel?" I asked Elizabeth.

"Where is he always?" she replied. "Go to him. Just hurry back, I beg you."

———

I found Samuel at the barn. He hunched over Nathan's stall. No longer was he filled with confidence. He looked worse than beaten. "I am so sorry." I hugged him as hard as I could. But it was like hugging a stone. He didn't lift even one finger to touch my face or my hand.

I pulled away from him. "I have a plan. I will go to Jebediah and the Reverend. I will tell them I borrowed Angeni's necklace. That it was me who tracked Tobias that night."

"They will not believe you, a colonial girl, tracked Tobias, a Hunter, outside the garrison's walls." Samuel stroked Nathan's mane.

"I will make them believe me. I will show them my bruises, my wounds where Tobias attacked and tried to kill me. They will punish me, they will put me in the stocks, beat me, but they won't hang me. They won't kill me."

Why wouldn't he look at me? Oh, no. Samuel blamed me. And he had every right.

"You cannot do that," he said.

"Why not? It will save Angeni. You and she can leave and be done with this place." *Please forgive me and take me with you.*

"I went to Reverend Wilkins and General Jebediah. I told them Tobias and I were hunting. That we argued, fought, I killed him, buried him, and took full responsibility," he said. "They did not believe me. This is entirely my fault."

"It's not your fault, Samuel. You can't say—"

"It is! I fell in love with someone I was not allowed be friendly with, let alone love. I courted you; I encouraged Angeni to help me. I shared my feelings about you with Tobias. Everything that happened is a direct result of actions I had no right taking."

"But we can save Angeni. You of all people cannot watch her die. She is a mother to you."

"We cannot save her. And I will not watch Angeni die."

"What do you mean?"

"I am leaving." He walked away from the stall.

Strike another blow to my heart. I couldn't stop myself. I slapped him as hard as I could across his face. He just took it, his head whipped to the side. He wiped a speck of blood from his lower lip.

Oh, no. I was the most awful person in the entire world.

"I'm sorry. I am so sorry! But you can't leave," I cried.

"I have no choice."

"Yes, you do."

"I do not. Malachi's a Hunter. If you and I leave together, he will figure it out immediately, and will hunt you. You must pretend to be Abigail. Play the game. Give it time."

"I've given it enough time." I bit my lip.

"Give it more. Perhaps, you will find your way back to your life in the future. You will meet a man from that time who loves you and can make a normal life with you. I cannot give you a normal life. Right now, I cannot give you any life."

Please don't go. Don't go!

He walked toward the door.

"You leave now—and you're no better than any guy I ever met in my real life," I said. "Who cares if you are a Wampanoag man, a 'Child of the Morning Light'? Does that count for anything, if you can't stick out a little darkness? If you leave now—you're just another self-centered, arrogant guy, who comes and goes as he pleases." I balled my hands into fists and tried to cover the shaking.

Please be real. Please be the guy who loves me forever.

He looked at me. "No matter what our destinies, I will love you forever, Madeline." And just like that he left through the small door. He was gone.

By the time I dragged myself back to Elizabeth's house, my eyes were nearly swollen shut from the tears I cried.

CHAPTER 32

The next day, Elizabeth, who looked ready to pop at any second, and I huddled together with the rest of the garrison's residents in the commons waiting for Angeni's punishment. It was another packed crowd. I was surprised they weren't selling popcorn or refreshments. I prayed for a miracle.

Elizabeth wrapped her arm around my waist. "You should not be here."

"Angeni didn't hurt a soul. How can I not be here, knowing she's dying for something I caused? It's not right. Not fair. I have to say something."

Elizabeth pinched my arm. "No," she hissed. "They will arrest you and imprison you. They will state that your crimes are many: accessory to murder, lying, conspiring with the enemy, sedition, and treason. They will pay witnesses who will testify the only reason you were spared that day at the Endicott settlement was because you are a spy for King Philip."

"But that's not true," I said. "I woke up and found everyone dead, and the settlement torched."

Elizabeth shook her head. "They need a villain to pin all their regrets and remorse upon. They need a sacrificial lamb to make them feel better, and take away their pain. Right now, that person is Angeni. If you say anything—that lamb will be you."

The crowd parted respectfully, as Jebediah, Reverend Wilkins, and Malachi walked from the church through their midst, and took their places next to the hanging platform. Jebediah looked resolved. The good Reverend looked almost gleeful. And Malachi? Grief and darkness emanated off his body, off his soul. I felt it from almost twenty feet away.

Two colonial soldiers dragged Angeni from her holding cell, through the commons. She staggered after them, her arms tied behind her back. People yelled and hollered.

"Justice for Tobias!" A middle-aged colonial woman spat on Angeni as she stumbled.

"Kill the heathen witch!" another enlightened soul said.

The soldiers led Angeni to the hanging platform, and hoisted her onto it. Poked her until she climbed onto a stool. Her silver hair flowed freely down her back. She didn't cower or shake. She wasn't a victim's victim.

The hangman, who happened to be the same guard who wouldn't let me out of the gates to see Samuel that day he rode Nathan, secured the noose on the thick rope around Angeni's neck.

My heart was breaking. I couldn't watch her die for a crime that Samuel and I committed. Samuel wanted me to pretend to be Abigail, to hide from Malachi. He also wanted me to go home, and find some boy to fall in love with in my life back in the future. Unfortunately, neither was going to happen.

Reverend Wilkins admonished the crowd so he could speak. "Angeni has been found guilty of the crime of plotting, planning, and murdering a young man, Tobias, son of

Malachi, advisor to myself, General Jebediah Ballard, and friend to every colonist who fights the evil King Philip. She has been sentenced to death by hanging."

Loud cries of encouragement spiked through the crowd. My knees felt like Jello, and I must admit, I clutched poor Elizabeth's shoulder to continue standing.

The wind picked up and Angeni's hair swirled around her. She looked peaceful and loving; like an angel with a rope around her neck.

"Kill her, kill her, kill her!" The chant rose amongst the colonists: men, women, and children as they thrust their fists in the air. They were a mob now. An angry, hateful group that only wanted blood. It didn't matter that it was the blood of an innocent.

Elizabeth whispered. "She is prepared to die. She knows this mob would not only kill you in a heartbeat, but hunt down Samuel as well. They would cheer as they hang him, his feet twitching in the air. Is that what you want? Is that what you want for the boy you love?"

"I *will not* desert her!" I broke away from Elizabeth's side. I shoved, and pushed my way to the front of the hanging crowd.

"I would speak for Angeni." I put my fists on my waist to steady myself, stood up straight, and glared at Jebediah, the Reverend Wilkins, and Malachi.

Jebediah looked at his nails, like he was contemplating getting a manicure. The Reverend sneered. But Malachi nodded.

"Angeni is the most loving and giving person in this entire garrison. She has helped everyone here. Never hurt a soul."

Angeni shook her head.

A guy shouted, "Hang the Native witch!"

"I say we string up Abigail, too!" A woman yelled.

I swiveled and faced the crowd. "You colonists left your homeland to have religious freedom. You want to kill an innocent woman, and yet you have the audacity to call yourself God-fearing? You are only vessels for anger. You should have stayed in the lands where people punished you for your beliefs. Because in this new land, you become the same people who persecuted you."

"*Kill her, kill her, kill her,*" the chant rose amongst the colonists, men, women, and children as they thrust their fists in the air.

"No! I killed Tobias!" I screamed at the crowd and ripped the neckline of my dress open to show them my wounds. I knew the punctures were red, spotted with blood, and that my neck was more black and blue than flesh-colored. "He tried to murder me. Do not hurt Angeni. Punish me!"

"Your wounds are divine punishment for wearing a heathen necklace," the Reverend Wilkins said, and nodded at the hangman.

"No! It's my fault! Punish me!"

Jebediah and Malachi leaned into each other and whispered.

Angeni said, "Madeline!"

I turned to face her but not before Malachi tilted his head and gazed at me. His eyes turned black, and the muscles in the front of his neck tightened like cords that had been pulled too tight.

He knew I was telling the truth. I could feel it. He knew I helped kill Tobias. He knew, and he would try to hurt me. But I didn't care.

I faced Angeni. Her blue eyes were clear, and she smiled. "Madeline, life goes fast. Right now, we need to be just like life. *We need to go very, very fast.*"

My entire body tingled. I saw past the silver hair, the weathered face. "Mama?" I asked. "Mama, is it you for real?"

The hangman kicked the stool out from under Angeni's feet. Her body dropped. I screamed, "No!"

But my cry was drowned out by a guttural, massive roar made by a hundred of King Philip's warriors who surged over the garrison's walls.

CHAPTER 33

$\mathcal{F}$laming arrows arced over the walls, landing on buildings, roofs, and haystacks starting fires. There was a cacophony of shouts and yells, cries and screams, as Philip's warriors scaled the top of the garrison's spiked, wooden fence like it was made of matchsticks. Most of the Native men dropped to the ground below, and started swinging their knives and hatches. Those perched on the top of the fence released another volley of arrows.

The colonists screamed and scrambled for cover or their weapons. Mrs. Powter fled toward the church. Daniel and a few of his friends were already armed and fired back at Philip's warriors. They downed a few, but it seemed fruitless. Not only had the warriors breached the fence, but they'd also opened the gates from the inside, allowing more men to run yelling, and screaming inside.

I swiveled my gaze toward the hanging platform on the tiniest chance there was a miracle and Angeni was still alive. *But there was no sign of Angeni.* Her body wasn't even there. The noose lay on the platform floor. A small white bird fluttered next to it and then, with great effort, flew into the air, dodging the arrows and the gunshots.

A burning arrow skimmed the skull of Angeni's hangman, and the guy's hair started on fire. Seemed King Philip had chosen just the right moment to take everyone off guard and launched his attack.

They weren't here for a Thanksgiving celebration, or a tea party. Left and right, I watched the colonists drop like flies, their bodies jerking, falling, collapsing. Gunshots blasted and colonists, as well as Natives, staggered and fell clutching bloody holes in their bodies. Then, there were the knives and hatchets. A jugular cut; a knife through the heart, a neck severed.

I should have been freaking out, but this almost felt familiar, like déjà vu. Like, I'd been through this before. The hangman screamed as a warrior leapt on him. They landed hard on the ground, fist fighting, and grunting. Jebediah grabbed a rifle from one of the guards who lay dead, pulled up and fired at the warriors.

Elizabeth. Where was Elizabeth? I looked over to where we were standing, and spotted her kneeling on the ground, her hands clamped over her head. I crouched, and ran to her side. "We have to hide, Elizabeth. Or run!"

She grabbed my hand, and I hoisted her up. When Reverend Wilkins pushed in front of us, knocking us to the side. I grunted, and barely managed to keep Elizabeth from falling. A warrior buried a hatchet in the Reverend's back, and his blood spattered across Elizabeth's face, dress, and my hair, as the good pastor collapsed, twitching, on her shoe.

Elizabeth froze, and her face morphed into a mask of terror. I yanked on her arm, and dragged her with me. "You are not allowed to freak out on me! I know where we can hide."

I looked around for the squat tree trunk that covered the

tunnel that led to the outside of the garrison. I spotted it: thankfully, it wasn't that far away. "Hurry!" I pulled and pushed her massively pregnant self through the arrows, skirting the fires, the bloodshed and mayhem. Miraculously, we were not hit.

"Where is Jebediah?" She panted for breath.

Good question. "He is being a soldier, right now. That's his job. If you stay alive, he will find you."

The screaming and yelling continued around us, as we crouched low and inched our way to the tunnel. "Stay close to the ground," I said. "Do not move until I tell you to move."

I pushed the tree trunk aside. Good, the tunnel was still there. Even better—it was wide enough for a pregnant woman. "Get in."

"But…" She hesitated.

"Move!"

She lowered herself into the hole, while I gave her instructions, and impatiently waited for my turn to follow her. "We stay here 'till the battle is over. If they find us, we crawl forward. On the opposite end of this tunnel there is another opening to outside the garrison's walls. Do not call for Jebediah, or anyone, until enough time has gone by that you know for certain Philip's warriors are gone."

Elizabeth was nearly down into the passageway and I had one foot in when I spotted young Mary Smythe, crying. She patted the bloody, motionless body of a woman who lay on the ground, several yards away.

"Mama," Mary said. "Wake up, Mama. Please."

Just broke my heart again. "Stay down, Elizabeth," I hissed.

I ran for Mary and scooped her up. She sobbed and pummeled me with her chubby, little fists. "Where's my big brave General girl?" I whispered. Mary snorted back tears but stopped flailing and collapsed her head on my shoulder, her arms wrapped around my neck.

I lowered her down in the tunnel with Elizabeth. But now, there was no room left for me. And, I could tell by the look on Elizabeth's face that she knew that.

"Abigail?" She held Mary, patted her back, and tried to soothe her.

"I'll be fine." I pushed the trunk back over the opening. "Remember, even if you're very scared, don't cry or call for anyone, until this is all over." I paused before I covered it completely. "I love you, Lizzie. Thank you."

I ran as fast and far away from the tunnel as I could get. I didn't know where to go. And then I did. I headed toward the barn and ducked inside. I heard Nathan whinny. But Nathan wasn't in the barn.

"Messenger!" One of Philip's warriors shouted in a thick Wampanoag accent. "I seek the Messenger."

No way he would be looking for me. I was a sixteen-year-old girl, who had just been exposed to *the basics* of being a Messenger.

"Messenger!" the man hollered.

I peeked out the door, and saw an older, muscular, tattooed, half-naked warrior holding Daniel with a knife at his throat with one arm, while he held Nathan on a short rope lead with his other hand. I didn't know who looked more scared: Daniel, the horse, or me.

"What?" I asked.

"Show yourself, or I will kill your friend, Messenger."

My heart pounded, but I lowered my head, ducked out the door my arms in plain view at my sides. I wanted it to be obvious that I had no weapons. "I am the Messenger."

The warrior regarded me, his knife poised at Daniel's throat. He released his grip and shoved him. But Daniel just stood there and didn't flee.

"Go, Daniel! Please."

He turned and ran.

"I was told you would have proof," the warrior said.

What proof? I couldn't think of any powerful messages I might convey at the moment.

The warrior grabbed my arm and shook it. "Proof!"

I pulled back the top of my dress, and exposed my bruises and punctures. "These marks were made by a Hunter, who tried to kill me. I traveled here from many years into the future. I think in my lifetime, Angeni might have been called Rebecca. She was my mother. I am the Messenger."

The warrior grunted. He put his hands on my waist, hoisted me onto Nathan's back, and led us to a hole punched in the garrison's wall. It was large enough for a horse, a girl, and a warrior to leave the bloodiest battle I'd ever imagined.

CHAPTER 34

"*W*here are you taking me?" I asked when we were far enough away from the battle that the screams were muffled. But he didn't answer. Just pulled himself onto the horse in front of me, and we galloped off.

At first, I was repulsed, and didn't want to touch him. That lasted about thirty seconds until I realized—I really didn't want to fall off a horse. I clutched his waist. We rode for miles and miles. I hoped Elizabeth and Mary survived. I prayed Samuel was okay. Wondered if Angeni was really Mama, and why this guy was looking for the Messenger.

My entire short life in 1675 didn't prepare me for anything like this. Yes, I could now churn butter, sit in church for three hours, stack firewood, stoke fires, and chant Sa-Ta-Na-Ma. But being abducted in King Philip's War and taken prisoner? I had no training for this.

Hours passed. We stopped only once. It was already night and difficult to see. But the warrior still wrapped a rough rag around my eyes, and blindfolded me.

Soon thereafter, I could make out dim light through my blindfold, and I heard the low voices of people speaking

Wampanoag. I assumed we were at one of Philip's warrior camps. My abductor lifted me off Nathan, and someone led the horse away.

He tied my hands behind my back with some rope, and pushed me backward until I landed in a seated position, my back against a tree. "You, stay."

My heart felt like it was cracking open from missing Samuel. Where was he during the battle? I hoped he was safe and far away. My mind raced in circles wondering about Elizabeth and Mary in that tunnel. Did they survive?

I shivered, my teeth chattering. I heard hushed conversations around me in Wampanoag. Maybe I could find an opportunity, a way to escape. More likely, I'd be held captive for ransom like that poor pastor's wife, Patience Donaldson. Then they'd discuss why they'd even bothered kidnapping me, because except for Elizabeth, I didn't mean anything to anybody back at the garrison. As soon as they figured that out—I was history.

Maybe if I were lucky, they'd let me freeze to death. This wouldn't be the best way to go, but might be better than having my heart ripped out by some guy who thought that gesture meant he owned my soul. Only three people owned my soul: Mama, Samuel, and for the first time in my life—*me*.

My abductor untied the rope from my wrists, and the blindfold around my eyes. "I am called Nikana," he said.

I blinked and looked around. My eyesight was a little fuzzy, but I was at a camp of sorts, in a clearing in a forest. There were several small campfires, as well as a large one that a group of men stood around, and about a dozen makeshift thatched huts. Native people were everywhere: primarily men, but also some women.

A few stared at me for moments, curious, but most went about their tasks: cleaning and checking their weapons, giving first aid to wounded warriors and feeding themselves as well as the fires, so they wouldn't die.

There was also a child: a boy, about eight years old, gazed at me mesmerized. I didn't see any colonists. I didn't take this as a positive sign.

"Drink," Nikana said and handed me a container of water, which I downed immediately. He took back the container and thrust a small bowl at me. "Eat."

I stuck my fingers into the bowl, pulled out some chunks of meat, put them in my mouth, chewed, and swallowed. "Thank you."

He took the bowl from me and pointed back at the tree. "Stay." I did. He left. I was warm inside, but still freezing on the outside. I hugged myself, and rubbed my hands up and down my arms.

The boy sat next to the fire and played with an old-fashioned rifle. He got up, skipped toward me carrying the gun, and just about everybody in that camp dropped what they were doing and ran toward him.

He put a hand up in the air as if to stop them. They backed away and let him continue. Good. Not so good? Now I had about two hundred sets of not-so-friendly eyes staring at me, examining my every move.

The boy squatted on the ground next to me, dropped the gun, cocked his head to the side and peered into my face like I was an alien. "My name is Alexander. I am son of Grand Sachem Metacomet. What is your name?" he asked.

"My name is Madeline Abigail Blackford." What the heck should I say next? "I am the daughter of Raymond Blackford and Rebecca Wilde Blackford."

"Is your father a great warrior and king, like my father?" he asked.

"My parents are not kings of anyone, or any land."

Alexander was lean for a youngster, his cheeks a little

hollow. His dark hair was long, hung free, and rested on a thick fur pelt draped across his shoulders that was far too big for him. "Kings must go to war to protect their people and lands," he said. "King's wife and son must be proud of this, and not feel sad when King gone." He reached his hand out and touched my cheek with his index finger.

I didn't flinch.

"Where are your parents?" he asked. "Do they know you are gone? Do you miss them? *Do you think they miss you?*" There was a sudden stillness, as everyone strained to hear our conversation.

"My father's alive," I said. "But bad people attacked my mama and me. She fought them, but they won, and she disappeared."

The boy nodded. "Your mama was brave. Like a Great Sachem who saves his people."

I cried. I just couldn't hold back my tears any longer.

He wiped a few of them away with his thin little fingers. "You are cold."

I nodded. "Yes."

He yanked off his beaver cape and draped it around my shoulders, smoothing it around my torso, down my back, my arms. He leaned into my face, lifted my hair out from the cape so it splayed down the pelt. "Now, Messenger, you will be warm."

A pretty Native woman swathed in furs and necklaces swooped in, grabbed the boy's arm, and dragged him away from me, scolding him. She fussed over him, removed one of her furs and wrapped it around his skinny shoulders. He smiled back at me and waved.

Nikana latched onto my arm. "We go."

He led me through the camp. I saw guns and hatchets. I saw the wounded warriors lying on blankets, heard their moans and cringed. I didn't want to be here. Suddenly

Nikana deliberately tripped me, and I landed on my knees on the hard ground.

He yelled some words at me in Wampanoag: probably telling everyone I was a clumsy idiot. He bent forward, and whispered in English as he helped lift me back to standing. "Angeni sent word. Be yourself. Be honest."

What did he mean?

Nikana dragged me to the biggest bonfire in the camp surrounded by a circle of fierce-looking men. Some sat. Some stood.

"Angeni's traveler," he said, and bowed to a man sitting in front of the fire, who was surrounded by warriors. "The Messenger."

I stood in front of this group and followed all the eyes and faces that looked back and forth between me and the man. He sat on the ground next to the fire. He wore furs like everyone else, and a huge wampum necklace hung around his neck. He stared up and down at me: not with contempt, but curiosity.

His eyes were determined, fierce, but haunted. He looked like he had the weight of the world on his shoulders. People hovered around him, like flies.

Alexander skipped up, perched his chin on the man's shoulder, and smiled at me.

"I have been told you are a Messenger," the man said. "That you fly through time, and visit us from the past or the future. Do you know who I am?"

Alexander nodded at me.

"You are King Philip, the Grand Sachem of the Wampanoag Tribe," I said, and bowed my head. "You are the son of Massasoit, the Chief who helped the Pilgrims stay alive that first winter when they landed in the Americas, on his homeland."

King Philip nodded at me. According to the colonists,

King Philip was vicious, evil, demented. Now I stood directly in front of this man who was supposed to be a monster. But he didn't look that evil to me.

He looked like any important guy: a powerful man surrounded by dear family, friends, and people who did his bidding. Like any leader, his entourage most likely included people who plotted against him. Spies and jealous wannabes. Those who wanted to rise to power by taking his away.

Frankly, the murderous and hated King Philip looked normal. I realized if someone were going to kill me in the year 1675—I would prefer it would be someone like King Philip. At least I would leave this lifetime with dignity and decent karma.

CHAPTER 35

"*A*ngeni sent word to the Wampanoag Children of the Morning Light that we need to protect you," King Philip said. "While you train to be a Messenger, the Hunters realized you could one day be powerful. They seek to harm you. She asked if we would help keep you alive."

"Thank you." I felt relieved for a heartbeat, and then flashed on all the injured and dead people back at the garrison. Was that my fault as well? Nauseated, I clutched my stomach. "The attack on the garrison? Was it to save me?"

Philip shook his head. "No, Messenger. That is simply war. We planned that battle before Angeni sent us news about you."

"How did she do that?"

Philip gestured. From the back of the circle, Samuel stepped forward. I think my heart skipped and might have stopped for a few seconds.

"You're alive," I said.

"As are you," he said.

"This is why you wouldn't stay?" I asked.

He nodded. "Angeni had made up her mind to remain

with you. She said Malachi made her leave you before and she would not let him do that in this lifetime."

Angeni was indeed, Mama.

"She sent me to King Philip to ask for his help to guard you," Samuel said. "Because until you learn more about traveling, you are too vulnerable." He stared at me. His face was flushed. His eyes were clear.

Samuel didn't want to leave me.

King Philip cleared his throat. "Angeni did us a favor many years ago by raising Samuel when the Hunters killed his father, my friend. We return that favor by offering you protection. You will sleep here tonight. At first light tomorrow, Samuel and Nikana, one of my finest warriors, will journey with you to northern lands where there is no war."

We were headed for Canada. Before it was called that.

"They will try and hide you from the Hunters while you train there with a powerful warrior. He will teach you to be stronger, Messenger."

"Thank you King Philip," I said, and bowed to him. "Thank you for your kindness." Alexander raced through the crowd around the fire, wrapped his arms around me, and hugged me. I hugged him back. I swear I almost saw a hint of a smile cross Philip's worried face.

Samuel stepped forward, and took my arm to guide me away.

"Messenger," Philip said.

I turned and faced him. King Philip looked exhausted.

"Do you have any messages for me?"

I thought about it for a moment. This was my first message, and yes, it was a little nerve-wracking. But I had to tell him my truth.

"Yes," I said. "It's time to ransom Mistress Patience Donaldson and let her return to her family."

CHAPTER 36

*K*ing Philip gave Samuel and me a tiny hut where we could rest, and a few blankets. We lay on the ground, my head resting on his shoulder.

"I was scared I would never see you again," Samuel said. "You were so angry."

"I was. I didn't understand. I still don't understand what being a Messenger means. Why Mama and Angeni appear for these tiny moments in my life, and then leave. I couldn't imagine you leaving. I'm so sorry I slapped you. That was wrong."

"That was expected," he said.

"Angeni's...she's gone," I said. "I don't think she died."

"She traveled. She can do it consciously. She told me that if she travels while she is dying, she couldn't come back. I will miss her. She wanted to teach you to travel consciously as well."

"I want to learn." *If only I didn't have so many fears.*

He kissed my hand. He kissed my lips. I wrapped my arms around his neck. He kissed the wounds on my neck where Tobias tried to kill me.

He flipped me onto my back and pressed himself on top of me. I wanted everything. But he hesitated and pulled away. "I love you, Samuel. I want this."

"I love you, too. But I want this when we are not filled with anger, or fear. I want us to be together when no one attacks us. We know it is our choice, and not simply a way to pass time."

He was right. I sighed. "Then hold me until tomorrow."

He wrapped his arms around me tightly.

Nikana, Samuel, and I left King Philip's hideaway at dawn. Philip's people supplied us with water, food, and weapons: bows and arrows, knives, a couple of hatchets, and a gun. But no Nathan. Philip needed him for war duty.

I kissed that gorgeous horse good-bye on his snout. Nikana grabbed my arm and said, "We go now."

We walked quickly and quietly, heading north. We made our way around a large swamp. Nikana guided. I was in second position, Samuel yards behind me. I wanted to find our way to someplace, where Samuel and I could be together without war. I hoped Angeni was okay wherever she was. I was curious about the new mentor who was waiting to train me. But that person could never hold a candle to Mama.

We hiked for hours through narrow paths in thick woods. Passed a couple of smaller ponds. I pretty much stayed away from the water, as the anxiety would rise and start to close my throat if I got too close. After nearly being drowned—I now had a thing about water.

Sunset came and went. Nikana led us to caves close to the cliffs overlooking the ocean, where we could rest until sunrise. The air inside was musty. The waves crashed, muffled, far below.

Nikana lit a small torch so we weren't in complete darkness. The caves were narrow and lined with old rocks. The part we were in was tall enough to stand straight, although Nikana's head almost skimmed the ceiling.

I was exhausted to the bone. I think Samuel and Nikana were, too. I drank from a flask, but stopped myself from guzzling, as there was only so much to go around. I handed the flask to Nikana. He drank a small amount, and passed it to Samuel. We shared a meal of jerky and corn cakes.

"Should we keep going and try and get further away?" I asked.

"It is too dangerous to journey more tonight. You will never outrun a blood enemy," Nikana said. "But you can be smarter and more prepared than your enemy realizes. Samuel, take the first watch." He leaned back against the cave's wall and closed his eyes.

"Even a Messenger needs to rest." Samuel squeezed my hand. "We will journey fast tomorrow." He disappeared into the darkness, and I assumed he positioned himself closer to the cave's entrance.

I leaned back against the musty walls. At some point Samuel wrapped his arms around me and we slept.

I woke to guttural shouts. "No, Malachi!" Nikana cried out.

Samuel grabbed his knife. "Take the torch. Run!" He pointed in the opposite direction of the cave's entrance.

"Where?" My heart pounded and my hands broke into a sweat.

"Follow the path that leads upwards. Nikana told me there are other exits at the top. Go!" Samuel said.

CHAPTER 37

J stumbled through the caves, practically bouncing off its walls. The ceiling lowered and its width narrowed. At points, the rocks were so close together; I had to turn sideways to squeeze between them. In the distant background, I heard the most awful screaming.

The voice wasn't Samuel's. It was Nikana's death cry. Malachi was butchering him. I stopped, leaned my head against the cave's wall, grimaced, and covered my ear with my hand, as I tried to block out the screams.

And then the screaming stopped, and there was silence. Should I go back? No, no, I had to move forward. There was a glimmer of light ahead of me. I followed that to another opening into and out of the caves. My back against the wall, I peeked out at a forest, the sun rising through the trees on the horizon.

Now it was only Samuel and I left to battle Malachi, the man determined to kill me. We could not outrun him. It dawned on me that Malachi desperately wanted to kill me/Abigail not only for revenge—but also because Abigail was most likely my ancestor. *Abigail dies and I will never even be born. End of problem.* I got up off the ground and ran straight toward the sunrise.

A low-pitched droning penetrated my ears and rattled my bones. Being a city girl, I usually didn't care about a little noise. Could be an L train whistling nearby outside my bedroom window, a bus chugging down the street, or a garbage truck picking up trash on any normal day. But it wasn't any of those, 'cause this day definitely wasn't normal.

I tore through a thick wood, my breath ragged as skinny tree branches whipped across my face and body. One slapped my forehead and something warm trickled into my eye. I wiped it away and saw that my hand was bloody. I should be used to that by now.

But I flinched and tried not to cry out in pain because *he* was hunting me. If he heard, he would calculate how far away from him I was. Then he would know how quickly and easily he could catch me. And if he caught me, he would kill me.

But I didn't want to die, yet. Not here, not now. I had to find a way to be with my Samuel.

I started running again but this time shielded my face with my arms. My feet kicked up some dirt as well as a few yellow and orange leaves blanketing the ground.

I fled past ancient pine trees with thick, round trunks and branches covered with needles that towered over me like a canopy when I tripped on the hem of my skirt. I heard a loud rip as I fell toward the forest floor. My arms pinwheeled and momentum, possibly the only thing on my side right now, jerked me upright.

I stopped for a few seconds to catch my breath. The droning had grown louder. Good. I was closer to that place where desire, action, a little bit of luck, and magic would join forces. I'd find that moment to slip through time's fabric, travel hundreds of years back to the present and warn or even save people. Especially my Samuel.

Then I heard *his* voice, muffled, but close by. And his words chilled my soul. "Stop running, Messenger," he said. "You cannot save him or yourself. You cannot save anybody."

I'm sixteen-years-old and cop to the fact that in terms of life wisdom, people think teenagers have been through next to nothing. But recently I've learned the hard way that I'm not your *average* teenager, and wisdom cannot be measured in birthdays.

I also knew Malachi had more deadly warrior skills in his little finger, than Samuel and I had combined. It seemed just a matter of time before he caught and killed the both of us. Better me, than Samuel. I sank to my knees, dropped my head forward and waited for death.

"Hurry!" Samuel grabbed my arm and yanked me up. "You have to travel. Angeni knew you were a Messenger, and gave the last part of her life, here, to train you."

"But, I'll lose you," I said.

"No! You will never lose me."

"Madeline," Malachi called. "I won't hurt you. You are valuable to me. Just like your mama. Let me train you, and I promise; I will spare Samuel's life. That is a fair trade."

Samuel kissed me once, hard and fast on the lips. "Go. Run toward the sunrise, toward the morning light. Travel. You must try. *You have to try.*" He pulled away from me and ran back into the forest.

I raced toward the morning light. Really, was there anyplace else to go? I pushed through the forest and ran out onto a moss-covered, rocky precipice, on a cliff jutting high above the Atlantic Ocean.

The ocean winds swept past me. The sunrise nearly blinded me. I peeked down—I was hundreds of feet up in the air, above the shore. I thought of Angeni, and her lessons, and realized what I needed to try. Infinity. Life. Death. Rebirth. The clues were there all along.

I touched my fingers to my thumbs and chanted, "Sa. Ta. Na. Ma." I started spinning in circles, the same way I saw Angeni do in her hut, when Elizabeth nearly miscarried. "Sa. Ta. Na. Ma." I quickly grew dizzy. I hated getting dizzy. If I fell from this height, I would definitely die. But Angeni had told me that I needed to release my fear of letting go, my fear of being dizzy.

"Sa. Ta. Na. Ma." I spun in circles as the rainbow of colors from the sunrise washed over me. Their hues seemed to breathe life into the chant. I felt a force tugging at my soul. *"Sa. Ta. Na. Ma."* I spun in circles faster and faster as my arms reached higher and higher until they were over my head and my skirt flew in circles above my ankles.

"I think I'd recognize you anywhere, Madeline," Malachi said.

In a blur I glimpsed him draw his bow with an arrow aimed at me.

"Madeline, come to me," I heard Mama say. I smiled.

I'm coming, Mama. I'm coming! I'm learning how to be a Messenger.

I kept spinning on top of that cliff overlooking the ocean in the most glorious sunrise I'd ever experienced. I felt an arrow pierce my back next to my shoulder blade, and punch its way through my lungs out toward my chest. It hurt something awful. At the same time my soul ripped from Abigail's body. I flew high into the heavens and blended with the sunrise for moments.

I watched Abigail below me spin slower and slower, multiple arrows hitting and piercing her body, until she finally collapsed on the ground.

CHAPTER 38

I heard soft voices and my nose crinkled from a harsh antiseptic scent. Firm hands rubbed my shoulders. They felt like my dad's. A smooth, cool, gentle hand stroked my cheek. "Come back to us, Maddie," a woman said.

I blinked my eyes open and stared, groggy at a pretty woman's face. "Elizabeth?"

"Raymond!" Sophie jumped.

The shoulder rub stopped abruptly. I was in a room that was small, white, and blurry.

"Oh my God, Raymond, oh my…" Sophie said.

My dad's face loomed in front of mine. "Madeline? Talk to me."

"Daddy?" My vision focused. His hair wasn't combed, his T-shirt had stains on it, and his eyes were bloodshot and tired. He looked perfect.

"Yes, honey." He smoothed my hair back from my forehead while tears welled in his eyes. "Talk to me. Ask me anything."

"Is Samuel okay?"

"Nurse! Nurse!" Dad yelled. "Where's the dang emergency, call button?"

There was hospital machinery and an IV bag hung from a metal pole in this small, pristine, white cubicle. The furniture consisted of small, vinyl chairs and a skinny hospital bed that I lay on outfitted with metal guard railings. I was connected to monitors and tubes. A curtain separated me from the other half of this place.

I noticed what was *not* in the room. There were no autumn leaves, or smoke billowing from fires. No war cries, no gunshots, knives, or tomahawks. And no skilled, malicious Hunter determined to kill me. These were all good things.

But there was also no Samuel.

My waking incited a blur of activity. Techs and nursing assistants ran into the room. Some shone lights in my eyes; others took my reflexes: my elbows, knees, and the back of one heel. 'Cause the other one was in a cast up to right below my knee.

A nurse told my parents to leave the room until after the doctor checked me out.

"How long have I been here?" I asked her.

"You were in the hospital for two weeks," the doctor said and perused my chart. "You were transferred here about a month ago."

"I've been out six weeks?"

"Yes." She smiled at me. "But, now you're back. We're going to run a few tests."

After that I was scanned and probed, and poked for most of the day. It seemed pretty much everything turned out all right, because they allowed my family back in the room, including Jane.

Sophie squeezed my hand.

"Am I going to be okay?"

"You're going to be perfect." She smiled. "Who's Elizabeth? I don't remember her as one of your Preston friends."

"She saved me after the attack at the Endicott settlement. You know, during the war. You remind me of her."

Sophie frowned. "What war, honey?"

"King Philip's War."

"I'm blanking on that one," Dad said. "When was that?"

"1675."

He shook his head.

"How come I didn't get creamed on the train tracks?"

"There was a young man. He jumped onto the tracks and pulled you to safety. You were very lucky. You had a good Samaritan." Sophie said.

Oh my God. A "good Samaritan?" Could it be Samuel?

"So, um, what did he look like?" I asked.

"We don't know, kiddo," Dad said. "He disappeared right after he saved you."

An aide wheeled in a cart with a tray on it. Apparently I had to eat pudding, Jello and more liquid-based foods before they'd take out my feeding tube that was stuck down my nose. Very uncomfortable.

Jane leaned in, and examined all the food-like items on the tray. "Tapioca. Ew. Let me see if I can score some chocolate." She kissed me on the cheek and whispered. "I'm glad you're back." She left in search of better pudding.

Between the lemon Jello and the tapioca pudding, someone had placed a sprig of lavender.

"Could you call Aaron and Chaka?"

"We did. They're showing up here tomorrow."

"Oh," I said. "Did I tell you how much I missed you? Did I tell you how much I love you?" Everyone got a little weepy then.

I ate. I slept. I woke. The next day they took out my feeding tubes. (*Note to self: be grateful for small blessings.*) An O.T. evaluated my speech. Apparently, yes, I still talked too much. I hung out with my family while a P.T. did joint mobilization on my arms and legs.

The Doctor popped her head in. "Good girl. You need to exercise. Get stronger. You've got some metal in that ankle, but you'll be in a walking cast as soon as you get out of here. You broke a couple of ribs. But those are healing. You obviously had a hard blow to your noggin, and a scar on your forehead. But all your test results seem to indicate there is no permanent damage."

I touched my forehead and felt a small soft indentation. "I have a scar?"

"It's not that big. We're using medicine to help it fade."

Angeni had said, "Every Messenger needs a marking. Otherwise, how would other Messengers recognize her?"

"When can I go home?"

"If you keep doing this well, probably in a couple of days."

That afternoon the P.T. fitted me for a walking boot and showed me how to use the cane properly.

And then Aaron and Chaka walked in the door. Squee! It was a love fest.

"I love you. Don't hug me," I said and we tried to catch up. "Give me the dirt about the accident."

"You lay on the ground, and you were already unconscious," Aaron said.

"When this guy—" Chaka said.

"Sexy, a little older than us," Aaron interrupted.

"Literally jumped off the platform down next to the tracks. He grabbed you, hauled you up the wall and—" Chaka said.

"He pushed you back onto the platform and managed to

avoid the train, by seconds. But that's when all the commotion started."

"And he disappeared," Chaka said. "They had it on the news and everything."

"What did he look like?" I asked, hoping.

"Late teens, early twenties. Dirty blonde. Kind of a young Brad Pitt," Aaron said.

I had no right to feel disappointed, but I did. "Aaron, do me a favor please."

"Almost anything."

"I have memories about what happened while I was gone. I wasn't here, lying in a bed."

"Whoa," Chaka said. "Like you went someplace different, while your body was trapped in a coma?"

"Yeah. Can you Google King Philip's War? 1675, in the Americas?"

"America," Chaka replied.

"Yeah, but it wasn't called that back then." I told Aaron and Chaka about Samuel and some of our adventures. They were skeptical. Then Aaron went online. The more info he discovered about King Philip's war, the more excited they became.

That's how we spent the next two days, with the exception of me having P.T., and my psych evaluation, and therapy with Dr. Broing, who I nicknamed Dr. Boring. He kept insisting my memories of Samuel were just coma-induced delusions. So, I insisted on calling him Dr. Boring.

Aaron would find something on the Internet, bookmark it, and then read it to me. King Philip's War with the colonists during the years 1675-1676 was real. The sites confirmed Philip's ancestry, his ascent to power, his decision to go to war as well as the details on how that conflict played out.

We found a snippet of information about the garrison I

lived at in Rhode Island. The attack was brutal, but about half the colonists survived, and the garrison was rebuilt. I found Jebediah's name, but I couldn't find anything on Elizabeth.

We found a bunch of info about Patience Donaldson and her abduction. After King Philip ransomed and returned Patience to her family, she wrote about her experiences, published, and her book actually became a bestseller.

No matter how many times we Googled Angeni, or Samuel—nothing came up.

The day I was scheduled to come home, Aaron thought he hit pay dirt. "This isn't warm and fuzzy," he said. "It's not going to make you feel better."

"I'd rather know." I clomped around the room with my new cane, wincing as I tried out my walking boot.

"I found this on a website called webbooksdotcom. During an ambush in the summer of 1676, over one hundred and seventy three members of King Philip's tribe were slaughtered. His wife and son were taken prisoners. The colonists sold them into slavery to English planters in the Dutch West Indies."

I stopped walking and sat back on the bed. "I talked to his son," I said. "He gave me his coat. He was only eight-years-old."

"When King Philip heard about their capture, he broke down and cried out, "My heart breaks… Now I am ready to die." Apparently after that happened, all of Philip's fight left him," Aaron said. "His army was decimated and he returned to his home, still hating the English colonists, but knowing the outcome that awaited him. His wife and son were never heard from again."

"What happened to King Philip?"

"Are you sure you're up for this, now?" He asked.

"Yes," I said. *Absolutely not.*

"He was pursued and shot dead by a Native man, who was accompanied by a colonial Captain. He was drawn and quartered. They chopped off his hand, and gave it as a souvenir to the man who killed him. That guy carried it around in a bucket, and would make some cash by showing it to people. They chopped off Philip's head and stuck it on a pike where it stood on display in Plymouth, Massachusetts, for twenty five years."

CHAPTER 39

*I*nterestingly enough, it was a major land grab. At the end of King Philip's War, the east coast Natives lost their land, their lives, or their freedom as they were sold into slavery. The colonists had definitely won this battle.

I left the long-term care facility that day. I got home and all I could do was cry. Dad made me put on a coat; we went outside and walked for a little bit. But I just couldn't share with him.

Besides not being with Samuel, the hardest part was not knowing what happened to him. Did he survive Malachi? If so, did the colonists ship him, like they did most of the friendly Natives to Deer Island where he most likely starved or froze to death during that bleak winter? Or was he sold into slavery, like the rest of King Philip's tribe? Maybe he was one of the few Natives who escaped, and joined another tribe.

I wrote a couple of versions of King Philip's story. One was for Stanley Preston's history assignment on major land grabs. One was about my experiences about a girl who traveled back in time and experienced colonial life. The third I wrote for myself. So I would never forget. That version was all about Samuel, falling in love, and learning to become a Messenger.

About a week after I left the hospital, I grew tired of living my days in easy, pull-on attire and my nights in a rotation of sweaty, flannel pjs. I was exhausted from staring at the iridescent stars on the ceiling and reminding myself that breathing required not only inhaling, but also exhaling.

Maybe falling in love with Samuel really was fiction. Perhaps Dr. Boring was right; maybe Samuel was just a byproduct of my coma-induced delusion. He never existed. But then why did I remember so many details about him?

How his hand felt on my face? His rough skin, his touch firm, but gentle. *That didn't feel like a delusion.*

The intimacy of his fingers when he tucked my hair behind my ear. *Could I make up a detail that small?*

When he pulled me to him, leaned into my face, cupped my chin, and said, "Madeline. I do not care where you are from—the future, the past, a star in the sky. I will love you here, now. I do not care what people think. I will love you, forever, Madeline." And when he kissed me like I had never been kissed before.

Was it possible to remember these moments from a *delusion*? A guy that I made up?

No. It wasn't. He was real.

And I was done.

Done with the shrinks and the know-it-alls who said I was just a silly teenage girl who had a couple of accidents. *I'd figure this thing out for myself.*

I pushed myself out of bed, limped to my desk, and found

Mama's book under a deluge of paper handouts on rehabilitative exercises and homework assignments that I needed to catch up on.

Her handbook was still beautiful, but a little dusty. I wiped it off with the edge of my pajama top, grabbed a mini flashlight and went back to bed. Propped myself up, laid it in my lap, and opened it.

I focused the flashlight and carefully turned the pages. Some were earmarked, but not by me. There were pages that had text written in foreign languages; others with scrawled markings including doodles, maps and arrows.

Then there were those pages that were bunched, stuck together, and didn't lay completely flat.

I had Mama's handbook for almost a day before I fell off the L tracks. Why didn't I register any of this when Dad first gave it to me? I felt like I'd been sleepwalking through my life, when everything around me could be a sign, or even magic.

I searched the handbook for clues. About halfway through I spotted something. The letters were small, handwritten in cursive, and faded. I pulled the book closer and read them.

General Jebediah V. Ballard (1640 - 1690) married to Elizabeth Sophia Endicott (1654 to 1715)

Children:
  Abigail Constance Ballard (1675 - 1740)
  William Tobias Ballard (1678 - 1708)

It was Elizabeth! She was my great, great, to-the-nth degree grandmother. She was my ancestor, not Abigail. Which also meant she survived King Philip's attack. Maybe I'd never be much of a Messenger in this life, but maybe I helped save Elizabeth when I accidentally time traveled. Perhaps that was good for something.

I put my finger on the paper under her name. Something tiny, dull and purplish stuck in the binding shone for a millisecond. The flashlight flickered and then died.

No way! I smacked it a couple of times and it fluttered back on.

I aimed it directly on the tiny purple thing. It looked familiar. I pulled on the binding gently, carefully with a finger. I saw the edge of a tiny feather. I wanted a miracle, needed evidence, but could not, would not damage this book. Nothing budged. I remembered when Angeni told me to use less effort.

I eased the edge of my pinky finger between the pages, and created a miniscule opening. I clutched my healing ribs with one hand and blew on the binding.

My ribs hurt, but the pay-off was worth it. My breath revealed a few remnants of small, colorful feathers, long, coarse, black horsehairs and tiny, multi-colored seashells. I flashed to Elizabeth kneeling awkwardly on the floor as she picked up the remnants of the necklace Samuel made me after Reverend Wilkins destroyed it.

The necklace Samuel made for me. In the year 1675.

Samuel was real. Not a coma-induced delusion.

We had been together, for real. We had fallen in love, for real.

Several days later, I returned to Preston Academy. I'd been in a coma. On life support, off life support. My broken ribs and fractured ankle were mending; I still walked with a cane and knew I had fallen in love. But, whatever, 'cause my history teacher, Stanley Preston, didn't care about any of that.

He ambled up and down the aisles, passing out the assignment papers I had missed to the other students. He walked past me and smiled. "We are all happy to welcome Madeline Blackford back to Preston Academy after her strange accident at the L platform."

Aaron whistled.

Chaka hollered, "Yay!"

Taylor Smythe studied her fingernails.

I knew Mr. Preston was a bully, and I was a little shocked there was no full-blown attack.

"This week's homework assignment is inspired by Madeline. Please pick well-known figures in history that experienced near fatal accidents. Or do you believe they were botched suicide attempts? And if so, make a case for that. Ten page paper due next week on Friday."

Chaka mouthed, "WTH?"

I shrugged my shoulder on the side that my ribs weren't broken. But living in the year 1675 had shifted part of my spirit. "Excuse me Mr. Preston," I said.

"Yes, Madeline?"

"Do you have questions you'd like to ask about my accident?"

He rocked on his heels. There was the same, malicious glint in his eyes that I used to see in Reverend Wilkins' eyes back at the garrison. A look oozing with judgment. A look that confirmed he would try and make me feel awful, just so he could feel good.

"As long as you're offering. I'm sure your classmates would want to know, could even learn something from what went through your mind, before your… *accident.*"

"Absolutely," I said. "You know me. I'm all about getting the message out."

Chairs creaked as every kid in that class swiveled and faced me.

Loved the attention. *Not.* I cleared my throat. "Before my accident, I'd had a bad couple of days. My stepmom was taking off for a new job assignment. The guy I liked—well, we all know how well that worked out." I heard a few guffaws. "I was scared of heights from a different accident."

"You don't have to do—" Chaka blurted.

"She already agreed," Stanley interrupted.

I blew a kiss to Chaka. "You, Mr. Preston, made me realize a few things."

He picked up a powdered donut from a small white box on his desk. "That's what I love about teaching." He bit into it and crumbs flew.

"The day before my accident, you laid into me. Embarrassed me in front of everyone in class."

"I have to be strict as well as honest. I only want what is best for each and every one of my students."

"Funny. Because when we were alone in this room, you threatened my grades, my partial scholarship as well as my potential college opps. I think you did that because you don't like me."

He hacked a little, and massaged his throat with his index finger.

"I was definitely sad when I was up on that L platform. But I wasn't suicidal." I pushed myself to standing with my cane, and limped awkwardly toward the door, feeling the emotional weight of every kid in that room on my shoulders.

"Class is not dismissed yet," Stanley Preston said. He munched his donut defiantly. The powder rubbed off on his face.

"It will be by the time I make it to the door," I said. "If I hear *one* rumor that I tried to commit suicide on that L platform, I *will* file a complaint with the Preston Academy Board so fast it will make your head spin. Because while teachers deserve respect from their students, students deserve the same respect from their teachers."

Stanley Preston dropped the donut. It landed with a plop on the floor.

Chaka and Aaron started clapping. A couple more kids joined them. The bell clanged. And I left.

CHAPTER 40

I stood in Preston Academy's foyer and gazed up at Mama's pale, rose-colored brick on the very top of the wall. She didn't deliberately abandon me. She saved my life in so many ways. I thought of Angeni: how she taught me to let go, to finally live. Because I let go just a tiny bit, I was able to fall in love with Samuel.

I think she knew the second I landed in Abigail's life that there were more puzzle pieces that needed to be fit together than just the obvious ones. I tapped my cane on the ground, and made a decision.

I limped over to the tall, library ladder, leaned my shoulder against it and pushed it, one clompy step at a time, around the walls toward Mama's brick.

Aaron appeared at my side. "Really?"

"Yes."

"Okay." He stepped in and wheeled until it lay directly below her brick. He flipped the safety lock down and gestured. "Madeline Blackford. Risk-taker."

I handed him my cane. "Madeline Blackford: Finally alive." I climbed five steps. I paused and realized—I wasn't

231

freaked. About ten feet up I hyperventilated a little, and hung onto the railing.

Taylor Smythe said, "Hey, let's watch the freak show."

And to think I saved your life, and made you a General. *(Note to self: next life I run into your sorry soul I'm not going to be so nice.)* I climbed a few more steps. This was as high as I'd ever climbed anything. At least in this life. I white-knuckled the railings.

Chaka said, "You go, Madeline."

"Go, Madeline!" Aaron said.

The entire foyer was packed with students and teachers looking up at me. "Go, Madeline." The chant grew. It sounded like hope. I made it up three more steps. I was about fifteen feet up that ladder when the heat washed over me again.

Dear God. There was no way I could time travel or escape from this moment, even if I tried. If I climbed just three more feet, I could stretch my arm high over my head and touch Mama's brick. Then I heard his voice.

"Maddie!" Brett said. The chanting slowed. Then stopped. "I've been trying to get a hold of you, but your entire family keeps hanging up on me. You need to get down from that ladder, now."

I swiveled my head high up in the air and looked down at him. "Why?"

"Because I've known you a long time, and you're terrified of heights."

"Maybe not so much anymore."

Brett shuffled his feet, and still couldn't look me in the eyes. "If you have a panic attack up there, who's going to help you?"

Someone whose destiny I was meant to cross paths with.

"No worries, Brett. I won't be calling you."

I climbed the last three feet in seconds, reached my hand

out and touched Mama's brick. It felt warm and magical. It felt comforting, but exhilarating. It felt fierce, but honest. It was way better than I ever imagined.

I felt Mama's energy, her love, and her devotion. But I felt something a little more than I bargained for. Angeni's magic, as well as other energies, emanated from that brick right into my hand. Maybe there were more magical souls I was meant to meet on this journey.

By the time I'd gotten back down the ladder, half the people in the foyer were raising their hands to bump my fist. I smiled and giggled.

———

The cab honked twice curtly, outside our house. I grabbed my coat off the peg next to the front door, and pulled it on awkwardly. "Chaka's folks are having a gig," I said. "I'm going."

"Hang on. I'll drive you." Dad practically jumped out of the kitchen door. He'd been hovering lately. Which was getting on my nerves.

"No. I need to do things on my own. Like normal. Like before the accident."

"You sure?"

"Your face down here, please." I pointed to his face and then mine. He leaned forward, and I kissed him on the cheek. "Yes, I'm sure. I'll be home early. You know I hate these things."

"That's my girl!" He stood back up. "No superficial, trendy stuff for you." He pulled a twenty from his wallet. "Cab money."

"Thanks." I pocketed it. "I'll always love superficial, trendy stuff in small doses."

Club Magique had been hot for a while, tanked, and was now making a comeback since Chaka's parents bought it. They gutted it, renovated it, and hired the most amazing musicians for live gigs.

The cab dropped me off in front by the red velvet rope manned by a couple of beefy bouncers. I handed the cabbie the twenty, and scraped through my purse for a couple of ones to add to the tip. This is why I normally took public transportation.

The line around the club snaked for what looked like blocks. I wasn't even sure I'd get in. A cute, young, buff bouncer spotted my cane, and then me. "Madeline Blackford?"

"Yes."

"I was informed, under pain of death, to find and bring you inside," he said.

"You found me."

I was a little surprised when he lifted me off the ground. He carried me through the masses of partiers inside the loud, dark club toward Chaka's table next to the dance floor, which was in front of the stage. I didn't know whether to feel grateful or embarrassed. Okay, both.

"Chaka told you to do this, didn't she?"

He nodded. "She didn't want you overdoing it your first night out." He deposited me next to her table.

Chaka bounced off her chair, and tried not to hug me. "You're here! You're not going to regret this. What do you want to drink?"

"Seltzer?"

"Pellegrino with two limes, please," Chaka told the waiter. She looked styling and gorgeous as always.

"Once you're out of that walking boot we're going shoe

shopping," she said. "Nothing too tall in the heel department. Maybe some fun Pumas or low-heeled boots. You are not going to believe who my parents booked for tonight."

I glanced around the room. It was packed. The dance floor was already jamming. "I'm assuming someone very talented and cool."

"I'm dying!" She fanned herself.

"Where's Aaron?"

She pointed to the dance floor. He was dancing with some cute, young guy, and looked like he was having a blast.

Chaka's dad, Nick Silverman, a handsome man with a full head of salt and pepper hair, hopped on the stage and took the mic. "Welcome to Club Magique!"

The crowd roared. He beamed. "We are honored to welcome the amazing, the magical, the incredibly talented... Rapper Ro-Boy to our stage. Put your hands together!"

Applause erupted. There were whistles, foot stomping.

The stage curtain lifted, and there he was—the next hot, young dancing/rapping/singing talent. He smiled that awesome, toothy grin of his and waved. "Hello, Magique!" He and his band launched into one of his insanely popular signature tunes.

People screamed and jammed onto the dance floor.

"Isn't it incred?" Chaka asked.

I sipped my bubbly water and nodded. "Thanks for inviting me. I'm glad I'm here." And I was. I was happy. I hadn't felt this way in a while. I swayed a little to the music as best I could.

"This next one is for you lovers out there, who in spite of everything, still believe," Ro-Boy said, launched into Stevie Wonder's song, *As,* which featured the most romantic lyrics.

I froze. I knew this song. It was an exquisite piece of musical poetry about loving someone for an eternity.

CHAPTER 41

*T*here are many names for the face of creation: God, Yahweh, Brahma.... I believe this energy formed not only the universe and our earth, but also inspires stunning pieces of art, books, and songs that make you weep.

I think this same force gave birth to two souls who were meant to be together, no matter what the year or circumstances they were born into: *Samuel and Madeline. We were destiny's lovers.*

I knew we could be with other people. Date them, care for them, and even make a life with them. But there would always be something slightly off. Something that didn't quite fit.

The party rocked, the music jammed, people danced, laughed, posed, flirted, and had a great time. But I wasn't one of them. I missed Samuel so much I felt like I lost a part of myself. "I'm going home," I yelled at Chaka over the music.

"I'll go with you." She pushed back her chair and jumped up. "Let me tell Aaron."

Aaron was still dancing with the cute boy.

"No. Don't. He's having a blast." I grabbed my cane that

hung from the side of my chair and made my way to standing. "Besides you need to stay. It's your dad's party."

"You shouldn't be out alone," Chaka shouted over the club noise.

"Because I'll turn into a pumpkin at the stroke of..." I looked at my watch. "Ten p.m.?"

"No. You're just not healed, yet."

"I'm healed enough to walk outside the front door and ask the doorman to hail me a cab."

"Fine. Call when you get home." Chaka threw me a kiss. "Love you."

"You, too."

I walked out the club's front door and shivered as a blast of chilly Lake Michigan air hit me. The doorman noticed my cane. "You need a ride, miss?" He lifted his arm toward the line of cabs.

"No, thanks," I said. "My P.T. says I need to walk more."

"You sure?" He glanced up at storm clouds bumping up against each other in the night sky. "It looks like rain."

I smiled at him. "Who's scared of a little water?" I limped off and left the pulsing beat of the club, and its bright, flashing lights behind.

I walked through Chicago's deserted urban streets on this chilly, windy, autumn evening that soon would turn into winter. I limped past mom and pop businesses closed for the evening, as well as the occasional trendy store with a cool window display, trying to grab a little attention in a changing neighborhood.

All featured thick, metal, accordion-style, ground-to-ceiling, security gates. You lived in a tough town and you learned, sometimes the hard way, how to protect yourself.

Most practical people would argue that a girl my age shouldn't venture out on her own in a big city at night. That my behavior would be tempting to thieves, bad guys, and other opportunists who preyed on people they thought were weak, or vulnerable.

Normally, I would agree with them. But, after everything I'd been through during King Philip's War, I thought: *Go ahead. Mess with the weak girl. Bring it flippin' on.*

I passed concrete and brick walls, separating stores from houses, streets and alleys. Many were tagged with gang graffiti. Seemed like someone was always calling someone else out. Were the results of these bitchy, turf disputes good for anybody involved? I wondered if even an experienced Messenger could get that message across.

The fog was thick, rain sprinkled, and a few snowflakes wafted through the air. My sides ached where my broken ribs were knitting, and my ankle throbbed. I stopped for a moment, bent down and tried to rub it, but couldn't do much with the walking boot still on. The lights that hung over my destination glowed yellow. They were high above my head, next to the L platform in the near distance. I willed my aching, body parts to keep moving toward them.

The rain tumbled down harder, soaking my hair. I attempted to walk around all the shallow puddles on the concrete. I no longer trusted pools of water.

I would never be with Samuel during this lifetime. There would be no looking up into his beautiful, proud face. No feeling his strong arms wrapped around my waist, hearing his laughter, or seeing the joy in his eyes when he gave me that necklace. Never in this lifetime would I feel his lips kissing my neck, my lips.

That hurt far worse than any fall I would ever take, any bone I would break. That knowledge ripped my heart into a thousand pieces. But in order for me to get on with *living* in my current lifetime, I had to come to terms with the fact that the love of my life existed over three hundred years in the past. Samuel wasn't the kind of guy who would want me to be unhappy.

I needed to let *us* go. That was the only way I'd perhaps find a smidge of happiness, let alone a little peace. Maybe, wherever Samuel was, he'd feel that way too.

I paid my token at the CTA's automated booth, and pushed through the turnstile. In front of me was a steep staircase. I sighed but climbed it. Clunk. I put my cane on each step above me before I hoisted my healing leg up. Clunk, another step.

I reached the top, walked a few steps, and paused under a thin, ugly, metal overhang to escape the rain for a bit. I took a few moments to regain my breath and glanced around the platform.

Gosh, it looked so different from that day six weeks ago, when I fell off and hit the ground. There were only a few people waiting on the train on this side of the tracks. An older lady read a book. A guy yapped non-stop on his cell telling someone about the importance of estate planning.

Two trains approached the station from opposite directions. They screeched and sparks flew off the rails in the near distance. On the opposite side of the tracks, the train was headed north. The southbound train was further away from the station: that was my ride, and would drop me close to home.

Time to get this over with. I limped out from under the

weather shelter into the pouring rain and faced the L tracks, just feet away. I pictured Samuel and me on that rocky cliff overlooking the Atlantic Ocean at sunrise. I concentrated and spoke my words to him silently, in my head.

Samuel. I am honored that I fell in love with you, a gifted healer, a Wampanoag man, a Child of the Morning Light.

My hands started shaking. Dear God, I was doing it; I was letting him go.

CHAPTER 42

*T*he trains screeched, but I closed my eyes, and concentrated.

Samuel. You gave me more love and respect than anyone I've ever met. But, I would be a rotten love, as well as a terrible friend, to keep you to myself.

If your bones are dead in the earth, Samuel. If your spirit is in a strange land, feeling lost. If your heart wavers because you want to love again? Know that I want you to go, and live another day. 'Cause I will love you, always.

I dropped my head in my hands, and sobbed.

As destiny would have it, the train heading north arrived first. A few people exited. The commuters huddled under the metal overhang on the opposite side of the tracks, covered their heads with briefcases, newspapers, or their hands, and hustled onto the train.

Its doors were closing, when a tall, lean, young man burst out of the stairwell and raced toward the train. He wore jeans, a dark coat, and had a backpack slung around one shoulder. His wet, longish, black hair obscured his face.

He slammed his hand in between the train's doors,

squeezed into the compartment, and took a seat on the side of the train closest to my side of the tracks.

I couldn't help myself. I stared at him through the train's faded, bleary windows. He set his backpack on the empty seat next to him, reached one hand up and smoothed back his wet, black hair. My gaze was drawn to the back of his hand. It had some kind of marking on it.

I squinted. It looked like a tattoo of a rising sun. My heart pounded. I limped closer to the platform's edge, and squinted at him.

An older, female, grizzled voice behind me said, "Honey, don't get too close to that edge. I heard on the news, a girl got pushed off this very platform, just weeks ago."

The southbound train whistled as it approached the station. Soon, I'd be on board; quickly and safely transported to just blocks from my home, and my family.

The northbound train headed out of the station. I felt the weight of someone's eyes on me. I turned. It was the boy with the dark hair and the tattoo. He'd pushed his wet hair back from his face and he gazed at me, mesmerized, through the window.

It was Samuel. I blinked. It was Samuel. I froze.

It was Samuel. And he was alive—right here and now.

"Samuel!" I screamed. He jumped out of his seat and pounded on the inside of the L train doors trying to open them, never breaking eye contact with me. "Samuel!"

But his train only picked up speed and carried him away from me, somewhere north of Chicago's downtown.

My mind raced, my skin tingled, and my head whirled. *I had to find him. If I worked really hard, I could find him. And we could be together, in this lifetime.*

My train was pulling up to the station. Should I get on it and go home? Should I cross to the opposite side of the tracks, and wait on the next train going north?

"Messenger!" A man yelled. He stepped out of the shadows on the platform across the tracks from me. He was tall, lean, older man with a full head of black hair. He wore a leather, bomber jacket. His chunky, silver ring glinted in the yellow, station lights.

It was the same guy who approached me that day in the garage. It was the man who rammed our car over the edge of the tall parking garage and made my mama leave me. It was Malachi, the hunter who vowed to kill me.

"I think I'd recognize you anywhere, Madeline." He reached inside his jacket and pulled out a knife.

And I realized—*this journey was far from over.*

Dear Reader: Thanks for reading THE MESSENGER! I hope you love Madeline and Samuel's romantic adventures. Their love story through time continues in **THE ASSASSIN #2.**

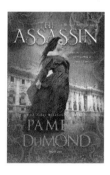

Madeline discovers that her true love, Samuel, is alive in present day, but doesn't remember her from their past. She journeys to a deadly royal conflict in medieval Portugal hoping to rekindle his memory.

Mortal assassins as well as dark-souled time travelers seek to kill them. Will Madeline and Samuel be together again in life—*or only in death?* "**The adventure of a lifetime...**" The Bewitched Reader. **1-click** The Assassin #2 or turn the page to read an excerpt.

Looking for more heartfelt reads with a touch of adventure?

Check out The Story of You and Me . Turn the page to read an excerpt. "It is a beautiful story that **made me believe**

in the power of true love and the miracles it can bring you." Summer's Book Blog

Sign up for my NEWSLETTER to get release info, news on sales, upcoming books, games, etc. Like my Pamela DuMond Author page. Join my reader's group on FB at Pamela DuMond's Dirty Darlings.

Happy reading!

Xo,

Pamela DuMond

EXCERPT OF THE ASSASSIN

THE ASSASSIN

MORTAL BELOVED: BOOK TWO

Before

Every place I journeyed had beauty as well as darkness; all my time-travels were bittersweet.

No matter the year, I met people with kind hearts who fed, sheltered, and even protected me from those who would harm me. But not everyone was kind.

Cunning folks sought to use me, paid me to spy for them, uncover their enemies' secrets; even deliver their very lives on a platter. And then there were the Hunters who tried to seduce me to their side or kill me because I was a Messenger: a breed of human who could slip through time's fabric into the past and deliver messages that could change one life or many.

Catapulting into the past was filled with unknowns and felt terrifying. Yet in this sea of chaos, there was a beacon of hope, an unwavering presence, one constant that made me fight to be a better Messenger, stay alive, and time travel yet again.

His name was Samuel.

I found him in almost every year to which I journeyed. I knew him no matter what style of clothes he wore, the length of his hair, or the tone of his skin. Whether he was rich or poor, from a favored class or a servant, I recognized his eyes, his smile, the sweetness in his soul; *but he never remembered me.*

I was a Messenger: I kept the memory of all our encounters, our lives, like a locket that rests on the skin and bones covering my heart. But Samuel was a Healer: he didn't time travel. His kind lived, died, re-incarnated and he didn't retain memories from his past lives. Every year I landed in required starting our relationship over: from ashes, from scrap.

"Oh, hello," he'd say. I'd glance around and find him. His eyes lingered on me and he'd be happy, or frustrated, or whatever the emotion was in our 'cute meet' during the year and drama selected by the gods and/or the fates to play out.

At first I thought our relationship was a dream. But our longing, love, and all the insanity that kept happening around us, between us—I felt in my bones like it was meant to be forever.

Every glance we shared, every adventure, each time we fought or kissed, and even the times we fell in love, were like facing the sky during the winter's first storm. You'd tilt your head back, catch a snowflake on your lips, and hope that this time it wouldn't melt, but melt it always did.

But I would not give up hope.

One day I'd travel to a lifetime where Samuel would remember me. He'd utter the very same words he said in the year 1675 when he pulled me to him and cradled my face in his rough palms. "Madeline. I do not care where you are from—the future, the past, a star in the sky. I will love you here, now. I do not care what people think. I will love you in the past. I will love you in the future. I will love you forever."

And maybe? Maybe if I worked very hard and learned how to be a better and stronger Messenger? Maybe someday Samuel and I could be together, for real, for good.

Chapter One

I stood on top of the "L" platform, the cold rain drenching me as the train carrying Samuel sped away from the station. "Samuel!" I screamed.

He gazed at me from the inside of the subway car and pounded on its yellowed window.

I'd come here to let go of the boy that I'd fell in love with hundreds of years in the past. I returned to the place where I'd been pushed in front of an oncoming train to release heartbreak and set both of our souls free. But Samuel lived and breathed just like he did when I first fell in love with him in the year 1675. He still had black hair, high cheekbones, and full lips. My mind flipped back and forth between awe and disbelief that he was alive, not just hundreds of years in the past; *he was alive here and now*.

"It doesn't matter what year you've traveled to, the clothes you wear, or who you pretend to be. I know you, Madeline. I'd recognize you anywhere," a man said.

I looked up and spotted Malachi standing across the tracks on the opposite platform. "Unfortunately, I can say the same about you," I said. Malachi was the fierce Hunter who tried to kill me in several lifetimes. He pulled a knife from his jacket and it appeared like he was going to try again.

Just when I thought the most dangerous part of my journey was over.

The few commuters that exited the train scurried off like rats abandoning a sinking ship. One woman punched 911 on her cell. "There's a guy threatening a teenage girl on the "L" platform at The Merchandise Mart." She looked back at me somewhat regretfully before she hurried down the stairwell. "I think he has a knife. Yes I can describe him. He's mid forties…"

"You're going to kill me, Malachi?" I asked. "A powerful Hunter is going to take out a teenage girl when she's alone at night. How courageous."

"You mock me, Messenger?" He asked. "I have bent over backwards to be patient with you."

"'Patient' like when you slaughtered the warrior who guarded me? Or 'patient' like when you launched a dozen arrows at me on the cliff overlooking the ocean?"

"You're sixteen now, Madeline. You've come of age, you're officially a Messenger, and you're fair game. Besides, do you really think anyone cares about your silly fantasies besides you?"

"My fantasies?" I hissed. "I know what happened was real. I have proof. How dare you even approach me on my home turf? You had your chance when I was six years old, you tried again in 1675, and you failed. If you kill me now you'll become a party joke, Malachi, an embarrassment to your kind. Other Hunters will laugh and gossip about you for hundreds of years. No—make that thousands."

"You killed my son," he said. "You killed Tobias."

"Tobias tried to murder me more than once. I cried real tears for him when he died," I said. "We didn't kill him on purpose; I would never hurt anyone on purpose."

The rain lessened, but for a bustling city, the night was too quiet. There were no oncoming trains, no commuters huffing their way up the steps to create a distraction. I gritted my teeth. "I'm leaving. I don't have time for your ridiculous behavior." I turned and limped down the "L" platform, my foot encased in the walking boot making embarrassing clomping sounds with every step.

I heard the whistle of Malachi's knife as it flew through the air. I threw one arm over my head and ducked when strong hands seized my waist, pulled me tight to him as we tumbled onto the ground. The knife flew high in the air, missed us by miles, skimmed the tall metal fence, and clattered onto the street below.

"You're not killing Madeline today, Malachi," A strange man said as he held me in his arms. "And you cannot kill her unless she breaks the rules or crosses the treaties. That will not be happening for quite some time, and trust me, it won't be on my watch."

My leg encased in the cast lay twisted underneath me. I winced and peered up at my rescuer: he appeared a few years older than me. "Who are you?" I whispered as he helped me to standing.

"Ryan! I'm happy to see you again," Malachi said. "I'm a little surprised to see you protecting the girl, but you are a worthy adversary. Like always, I expect this will be a delightful adventure."

"Go back to your hole in time, Malachi!" I said. "Where I hope you suffocate and die!"

"Where are your manners?" Malachi laughed. "I'll see you soon, Madeline. I, for one, am looking forward to it." He scaled the metal fence, hurtled over the barbed wire on the top, and leapt off into the city's darkness below.

"Holy crap!" I said.

"Are you all right?" Ryan asked.

He was dirty blonde, blue-eyed, and handsome without being pretty. "No. I'm definitely not all right. Thanks for helping me. Wow. But…" I glanced down the tracks as the train that Samuel was on disappeared from sight. "He's alive. Samuel's alive in this lifetime! I'm sorry. Malachi's right—I have no manners. Your name is Ryan. What are you, I mean, who are you?"

"Yes, Samuel's alive, Madeline," he said. "Samuel's a Healer. It's part of the pact between the Maker and the original tribes. Healers don't travel. They re-incarnate."

"What pact? *What tribes?* How do you know this stuff? Don't tell me you're a Messenger."

"I'm a Messenger," Ryan said. "And I've been sent here to, well, mentor you for a bit."

"Wait a minute," I said. "You're the guy who pulled me from the train tracks after I was pushed in front of the train. You're my 'Good Samaritan.'"

"Guilty," Ryan said.

"You saved my life," I said.

"Only once," he said.

"Twice if you count the thing with Malachi tonight," I said.

"He was probably just being overly-theatrical," Ryan said. "He's a bit of a pompous douche."

I couldn't help but crack a smile. But Ryan just stood there looking serious, like trouble weighed heavy on his mind. "You want something from me don't you?"

"It's simple really. I just want to teach you easy ways to be a better Messenger."

"No-no," I said. "I'm done with that time traveling Messenger stuff. Samuel's alive in this lifetime and I need to find him." I clomped down the "L" platform. "Do I wait for the next train? Of course I wait for the next train." I slapped my forehead with my palm. *"I can't think!"*

"You've been given the gift of time travel and you're turning it down to follow a boy?" he asked.

"I've been given the *curse* of time travel and I'm turning it down to find someone I love," I said. "Thanks so very much for looking out for me. Seriously."

"Give me your phone," he said.

I yanked it from my purse and tossed it to him.

"I think you should go home tonight," he said and entered his details into it. "Go home, text your friends, try and get some rest, and we'll talk tomorrow, okay?" He caught up with me and handed it back.

"Thanks," I took it. "Yes, absolutely. I'll call you tomorrow."

Which made me a big fat liar. Because I'd call him when I was dead.

BOOKS BY PAMELA DUMOND

'HOT' ROMANCE

21st CENTURY COURTSEAN series

TYCOON: A 21st Century Courtesan Prologue (FREE!)

PLAYER #1

MOVIE STAR #2

BELOVED #3

ROYALLY WED ROM-COM series

Part-time Princess #1

Royally Wed #2

Part-time Poser #3

Royally Knocked Up #4

Royally Wed Box Set: Books 1 - 4

THE CROWN AFFAIR series

His Sexy Cinderella - A Crown Affair Series Prologue (FREE!)

The Prince's Playbook #1

His Majesty's Measure #2

The American Princess #3

The Duchess's Decision #4

The Crown Affair Collection: Books 1 - 4

The Mortal Beloved Box Set: Books 1 - 3

COZY MYSTERIES

ANNIE GRACELAND COZY MYSTERIES
Cupcakes, Lies, & Dead Guys #1
Cupcakes, Sales, & Cocktails
Cupcakes, Pies, & Hometown Guys
Cupcakes, Paws, & Bad Santa Claus
Cupcakes, Diaries, & Rotten Inquiries
Cupcakes, Bats, & Scaredy Cats
Cupcakes, Bars, & Rock Stars
Cupcakes, Spies, & Despicable Guys
Cupcakes, Screams, & Drama Queens

The Annie Graceland Mystery Collection: Books 1 - 4
The Annie Graceland Mystery Collection #2: Books 5 - 7

FREE
TYCOON: A 21st Century Courtesan Prologue
His Sexy Cinderella - A Crown Affair Series Prologue

SELF-HELP
Staying Young

ACKNOWLEDGMENTS

Many giving, loving people helped me create this book.

Thanks Lori Jackson for rocking the new book cover. Thanks to my author friends and early readers/editors: Rita Kempley, Deborah Riley-Magnus. Thanks to my editors, Ramona DeFelice Long and Arianne Cruz. Thanks to Regina Wamba at Mae I Design for her amazing photography featuring model Jenessa CE Andrea. Thank you to my family. Thanks Melissa Black Ford, Celia Boyle, Carrie Hartney, D.C., Ed Schneider and Debra Sanderson for keeping me sane. Thanks Monica Mason, Cheyenne Mason, Michael James Canales, Adrienne Kramer, Shelly Fredman, Julie Dolcemaschio, Joe Wilson, Sadie Gilliam, Andrew Goldstein, Kristin Warren, Robert Bernstein, Ed Schneider, Dave Thome, Jacqueline Carey, and Kim Goddard Kuskin. Thanks Jamie Duneier for reading my ms and encouraging me to write the screenplay.

I spent hours researching King Philip's War. But the book *King Philip's War: The History and Legacy of America's Forgotten Conflict* by Eric B. Schultz and Michael J. Tobias helped tremendously.

Thanks to my readers. I am grateful we are on this journey.
    Xo,
    Pamela DuMond

ABOUT THE AUTHOR

USA Today **Bestselling author** of *Part-time Princess* © 2014 and other modern fairytales, Pam writes sexy, steamy, and on occasion silly.

Her books have been optioned for Film/TV, licensed by Chapters Interactive Stories as games, and featured in *Glamour UK*.

A Midwestern girl at heart, a Doctor of Chiropractic, Pam landed in L.A. where she says 'No' to kale, 'Yes' to Cardio Barre, and 'What do you want now?' to her two ridiculously cute cats.

Sign up for Pamela DuMond's newsletter.

Like Pamela DuMond Author page on Facebook.

Join the reader group at Pamela DuMond's Dirty Darlings.

Follow Pamela DuMond on Bookbub for timely deals.

Stalk Pamela DuMond on Instagram .

For more information...

www.pameladumond.com

Printed in Great Britain
by Amazon